THIS IS THE HOUSE

On a picturesque West Indies island, the capital is dominated by the house on the mountaintop: the house that Jacques built. Premier Justice Antoine Jacques was divinely happy with his beautiful wife Julia and their son Raoul — until Julia was stricken with total paralysis . . . For years now, La Morte, as she is known, has been confined to her bed. Then, one day, she is found dead. And Quentin Seal, author of detective stories, is begged by Antoine to investigate . . .

SHELLEY SMITH

THIS IS
THE HOUSE

Complete and Unabridged

LINFORD
Leicester

First published in Great Britain

First Linford Edition
published 2017

A catalogue record for this book is available
from the British Library.

ISBN 978–1–4448–3420–8

1

This is the House that Jacques Built

La Morte lay in the house that Jacques built, in a high white room overlooking the staring blue sea. 'La Morte' was what the natives called the poor creature — for was she not as good as dead? — but Julia Jacques was her name, and she was the wife of the Premier Justice on the Island. She was English, but her husband was French and came of an ancient Creole line. He was ten years older than Julia and adored her. When, five years into their marriage, at the age of thirty-eight, she was stricken between one day and the next with this dreadful paralysis, he nearly went mad. Every doctor, every specialist within reach was entreated to give advice. They were interested, they were sorry: but it was hopeless. 'But how long can she live — like this?' he asked the doctor in anguish.

'She may well outlive you, my poor friend. There is nothing organically wrong with her, remember.'

'But it is a living death!'

'It's a tragedy,' agreed the doctor, before he hurried away to another case, for tragedy was his daily bread.

At first Jacques thought the weight of her frozen beauty would crush him, but gradually, as time passed he became inured to it. Passion itself became compassionate.

They had one child, a boy. It was bitter to think how happy and fortunate they had been until this disaster.

He took her to live in the house soon after the tragedy. He had built the house originally as a commercial venture to attract tourists or visitors to the Island. It was not strictly a house, just two flats, one on top of the other. A plain, square, two-storied villa standing in a courtyard. Actually, it was all inside a kind of castle, built by the Portuguese, who conquered the Island in the sixteenth century and constructed their fortress on the top of the mountain overlooking the natural harbour of Carib Bay. Long after Portuguese rule was forgotten, the fortress remained. Time passed, and the castle crumbled to a picturesque ruin . . . Till Jacques came along, and with uncommon sense used the substantial foundations for his modern villa.

Apostle Island was the most southerly of the Windward Isles; and Wigtown, its ramshackle capital, was dominated by the house on the mountaintop. It made a romantic residence from the outside, practical within. It was pleasant to lean on the ramparts and watch the little pink-and-green-roofed town sweltering below, or to stare over the other side into the blue depths of the ocean.

But, whilst romantic, it was not a paying proposition, and so Jacques installed himself and family in the upper flat and rented the lower to his sister-in-law, Hattie Brown. Maybe the visitors to Apostle Island found the walk up from Wigtown to the house an insuperable barrier. Certainly it required considerable fortitude even in a native Islander to negotiate those two hundred and thirty-five stone steps in the noonday sun, with balustrades to lean against and shady trees overhanging here and there.

But it suited Jacques, and after all, he was Premier Justice: he had a certain position to keep up. Apostle Island had belonged to many nations, but although it was at this time British mandated territory, for nearly a hundred years the civil code had been French. The population was polyglot, but mainly French, Spanish, English, Portuguese and American. The black inhabitants were descended from slaves originally imported from Africa, and they spoke their own varieties of French and English.

So La Morte lay in her narrow white bed, motionless, hour after hour, and only God and she knew what thoughts flickered behind the smooth, white brow.

It was some kind of a feast day when all the servants had a holiday and were out dancing on the other side of the Island. Her sister Hattie sat in a cane chair by her bedside, reading aloud to her a translation of Professor Hirsch's learned treatise

Mass Mesmerism and the Human Will. That was Hattie's choice, not Julia's, and every now and again she would pause to explain the meaning of some knotty bit of prose. Julia's eyelids flicked up and down in approval. She was just beginning to believe that there might be something in it after all . . . the influence of one mind over another . . . She had seen Hattie do things, with her own eyes. She had even proved it once or twice herself in simple little things, things of which she could not be absolutely certain. But how fascinating it was, lying here helpless, to try and exercise one's power, to toy with the idea of being able to direct people and make them do one's will without a word being said, without them even being aware of it. That would *almost* make her life worth living . . .

She opened her eyes. Father Xavier's round brown face smiled down at her from the doorway. The little parish priest visited her regularly. She looked forward to his visits more than anything. Religion was her only consolation. Once a week she took Holy Communion. Once a week she confessed her sins. Poor lady, you would not have thought it possible for her to sin at all, in her sad case; yet the priest was often closeted with her for an hour or more. Of course, it was a laborious process: he had to help her by asking innumerable tiny questions, for she had never wholly recovered her power of speech. She managed to gurgle out something in an uncouth sort of way, which her intimates understood, but no more.

Hattie rose contemptuously from her chair when he came in. There was no love lost between her and the priest; she openly ridiculed all he stood for, she being the type of atheist who likes to bait the clergy and corrupt the innocent. She exhibited the title of the book to his gaze, mockingly.

'I should not have thought that was a very diverting book to read to an invalid,' he said mildly.

'Oh, she enjoys it. Don't you, darling?' Hattie grinned maliciously.

The two women were sisters, but they could scarcely have been more unalike.

Julia still was lovely, her enforced lack of expression rather suited her calm and noble features, and the smooth coils of her hair were as palely golden as ever they were. Hattie was twelve years older than her sister, more massively built, with a shapeless figure now, shabbily and unfashionably clothed. She had a big, red face surrounded by tousled grey hair, and eyes — her only claim to beauty — set rather obliquely in her head, a pale but brilliant blue, amazing eyes like a Siamese cat's. It was a joke among her friends — whether she bred Siamese cats because she resembled them, or whether she resembled them because she bred them. Her voice, too, was feline: high and shrill, not unlike their piercing complaints.

'Yes, Julia's very interested in will-power. We've been making some little experiments — with quite remarkable results . . . Oh, we've not done anything to alarm you, Father Xavier — so far,' she added, smirking.

'It seems an unhealthy amusement to me — even dangerous. To meddle with people's individuality is infringing sacred rights, you know. It's unpleasant, bordering on the occult . . . '

'Well, well, I should never have thought you believed in such childish things. As for it being dangerous, I don't believe anything can be worse for my sister than boredom and melancholy. There are so few things left to give her joy that I hope you won't think it your duty to forbid even this simple pleasure. It's just play. She tries to make me do trivial things, or the cats . . . ' She waved her arm vaguely.

Forbearing to argue, Father Xavier waited politely for her to take her leave. As the door closed behind her, the priest sat down primly beside the invalid. Watching La Morte's eyes, he began to question her.

He knew her trouble, the sin of the ancient fathers: *accidie*. Fruitless despair weighed on her soul, pressed on her like a physical burden. She longed for death. It was difficult for the priest to comfort and console her. If only she would resign herself to God's will, to His infinite mercy . . . But her dependence was intolerable to her; she felt no better than a senseless mummy.

She was of no use to her family either. Nothing but a hindrance to her darling husband, her adorable son. If she were dead, they would be free. It would benefit everyone. But this death-in-life was a cruel torment. It wasn't fair . . .

He reproved, rebuked, and exhorted with all long-suffering and doctrine. Tears of self-pity ran out of the corners of her eyes. He leant forward and gently wiped them away.

'Ave Maria, gratia plena, Dominus tecum . . . ' The wooden beads of the rosary slid through his fingers.

Presently he rose to go. She looked at him beseechingly, trying to say, 'Pray for me. Father, pray for me.'

Perhaps he understood, for his small brown hand rested a moment in gentle benediction on the thick hair crowning the pale brow. 'The Lord be with you.'

As he opened the door a Siamese cat sprang past him into the room.

'Ah, naughty!' he exclaimed, and went after it, for he knew the fixed house-rule that no animals were allowed in that room unless someone was there to see that they did no harm to the helpless creature in the bed.

La Morte grunted disapproval.

'But I mustn't leave him here, my child, you know that.'

She mouthed clumsily, her eyes bright with meaning, and it dawned on him that she was trying to convey to him her belief that she had successfully willed the cat to come to her room. He hadn't the heart to ridicule the idea.

He stooped to pick the cat up and a black paw flashed out like a snake. 'Ouch! Spiteful little creature!' There was a gurgling titter from the bed. He glanced up sharply. 'You might will him to keep his claws in till I get him outside, if you can!'

Outside, he dropped the animal with a thud on the floor and aimed a petulant kick at him. 'Nurse!' he called, licking his scratched hand ruefully.

A woman, like an efficient little mouse dressed in a white apron, came out of a room opposite, nodded to the priest, and slipped quietly into the patient's room. Strictly speaking, she was off duty that afternoon. Her midday siesta was over, but before she went out there were certain things to be done for her patient, to keep her comfortable until her return. She smoothed the covers and turned the pillows under her head. The green jalousies she fixed at an angle that kept out the worst of the sun but let in the light.

'I expect he's very comforting, isn't he?' She always made the same remark after his visits, unaware how it chafed her patient. 'You always look happier after he's been.' There was no sense in telling the poor soul that it was a lot of Romish superstition. If she got anything out of it, she was luckier than most, thought the nurse. She was preparing a hypodermic syringe as she spoke. She pressed a spray of fine drops into the air. The delicate needle point pierced the self-sealing rubber top of the ampoule and slowly drew the liquid up into the syringe. She dabbed a little surgical spirit on Julia's arm.

'Miss Whitaker has promised to keep an eye on you while I'm out,' she remarked as she drove the needle beneath the skin, for she believed in distracting the patient's attention from these little operations, however painless. 'There!' she said, and wiped away a tiny spot of blood. 'Now you'll be all right till I come back . . . '

Prudence Whitaker was Hattie Brown's secretary. She had not been with her very long, but was already proving more efficient than Hattie had hoped — far more efficient than she looked, certainly, for she was a shy little thing, hiding behind enormous horn-rimmed spectacles.

She had landed on Apostle some time previously — no one knew why. Her story was that she was the daughter of a country doctor, who had died while she was still at school and left her nothing but debts. She had taken a post as governess to a family in Australia, and then after a time she had left there and gone to another family in Brazil, and then from Brazil — But suffice it to say that eventually she turned up, pretty well on her beam ends, on Apostle Island.

Goodness only knew what she thought of the peculiar household in which fate had flung her this time. The queer, disagreeable old woman, with her pets making free of the whole flat, and the dirt and untidiness everywhere . . . Not what one expected to find in an *English* household. Little dishes of food for the cats were to be found all over. Books lay in heaps on the floor till their bright covers were filmed with dust and newer ones took their place.

Prudence glanced at her wristwatch and frowned thoughtfully. It was sickening that it should be *today* . . . She filed away the carbon copies of the letters she had just written and carefully fastened down the cover of her typewriter. She slid open the table drawer —

A sound at the window made her swing round, hand on heart. A golden head pushed through the leaves tapping at the glass, and Raoul's dark, faun-like face laughed down at her.

'Oh, Raoul!' she exclaimed.

He pushed the window wider open.

'Did I scare you, miss?'

'You did for a moment. I was miles away. Are you going up or coming down?'

'Up. I am quite filthy all over. See? I must change and make myself beautiful again.'

Prudence looked at him meditatively.

'I wonder if you would do me a favour for once?'

He pouted. 'You don't say, 'Raoul, to me you are always beautiful'!'

'You would look more than beautiful to me if you would help me out. It's nothing much. Only, I promised Nurse that I would keep an eye on your mother while she was out this afternoon, and now there are these important letters to be sent by the afternoon post. I'm afraid Miss Brown will be annoyed if they don't go.'

He crouched down and swung himself into the room beside her. He was very lithe and attractive in his white flannels. Raoul Jacques was only about eighteen, self-conscious and spoilt, but indisputably charming.

'I could take them for you,' he offered.

'Well, I thought perhaps you would stay with your mother while I take them. You see, they have to be registered and so on. I really ought to attend to it personally. But if you would just wait with her till I get back, I should be eternally grateful to you.'

'Pooh! Eternally grateful because you can post some letters? Wicked Prudence, you are up to some mischiefs. Confess to me now!'

'I've told you the truth, you silly boy. What else would I be doing?'

'Who can say? Perhaps you go to meet a lover?'

'And perhaps I don't,' she said firmly. 'Your mind only runs on one thing.'

'If it is to meet a lover, I advise you to put some powder on your nose.'

She smiled equably and turned to the square of mirror above her desk. 'It *is* hot,' she agreed.

His tanned face laughed at her reflection. He grasped her firmly beneath the arms and kissed her neck fiercely.

'Oh, Raoul, please stop. It's too hot for that sort of nonsense today, really.'

'I see. My love is only nonsense to you,' he said huffily.

She powdered her face lightly.

'Don't be absurd, Raoul. As though you care tuppence about me!'

He surveyed her critically. 'You are really quite pretty without your glasses, you know. Why do you wear them?'

'To keep my boots clean, of course.'

'Ha, ha! Very well, take your letters and go. But do not be too long. I warn you, I too have an assignation.' He gave her behind a friendly nip and sprang back on to the sill.

'I do wish you wouldn't do that. It's disgusting, Raoul.'

'I do it to give you pleasure, you cold English girl; Women should be flattered by these little attentions.'

'It's the sort of vulgar monkey trick one might expect from Orlando . . . but *he* doesn't know any better.'

'Thank you,' said Raoul with dignity. 'So I am no better than a monkey — charming English manners! Good afternoon, miss.' He continued haughtily up the steps that led to his home.

Prudence laughed.

'Never mind, Raoul, you're a nice lad really. And you won't forget, will you? I'll do as much for you some day,' she called after him.

'Prude! Prude!' cried a high, distant voice; and her expression darkened as she replaced the clumsy spectacles and hurried from the room.

'Yes, Miss Brown?' Prudence gazed down with an unfathomable expression at her employer sprawling untidily on the divan in a faded cotton gown, an open book lying upside down over her stomach. It was the hour of siesta. The pale blue eyes slowly opened.

'Well, Prude, what do you want?'

'You called me, Miss Brown.'

'Did I? But you were such a long time coming that I nearly fell asleep. This is an excessively stupid book . . . it wouldn't keep a cat awake . . . Well? What have you been up to, eh?'

'I've just finished the South American mail.'

The old woman cackled ironically.

'So I noticed. That was why I called

17

you, I remember now. I wish you would not flirt with my young nephew, Miss Whitaker. It really is not suitable.'

Miss Whitaker flushed.

'Really, Miss Brown! Nothing is further from my intentions. I would be very pleased if you would speak to your nephew and ask him not to pester me with his attentions.'

'A liar as well as a prude, eh? Not a very likely story, my dear Prude. You're considerably older than he is, and we know that it is always the woman's fault in these affairs. We're not as simple as all that, you know. Besides, he's a very pretty little boy. *I* wouldn't mind, myself — ' She chuckled obscenely. Prudence bit her lip.

'Miss Brown, I know you're only joking, but I don't happen to find it amusing. And I should also be glad if you would not use that silly nickname for me.'

'Prude by name and prude by nature . . . I'm a horrid tease, I know. Sit down here, my dear, and tell me you're not really angry. I'm a silly old woman who gets bored and lonely. You may be like me yourself one day. What is there left for me in life? You're young and you've got your life before you. Have pity on a poor lonely old creature who has no one to love her.' She stroked the girl's bare arm absently. 'If I had married, now, and had a daughter — a sweet girl like you — how different everything would be. But the man I loved married someone else, alas ... And now I'm just a tiresome old nuisance, and you're wondering how you can get away, aren't you?'

It was uncanny how she always seemed to know just what you were thinking. Prudence simply loathed being pawed, and it required all her self-control not to pull her arm away. She gave a nervous little laugh.

'I'm sorry, Miss Brown. It was only that I promised Nurse I would stay with Madame Jacques this afternoon while she went out, and — and I'm late already. It's a feast day today, you know, and all the servants are out,' she explained.

'Well, whyever didn't you say so before, you little fool?' She released her grip.

'What are you waiting for? Run along, then.'

Prudence gladly hurried to her room, crammed on a shady straw hat, carefully locked all the drawers in her chest and dropped the key into her handbag and, with a last cautious look round, tiptoed discreetly down the interminable steps.

In the flat above, Raoul was talking to his mother through the open doorway that led from her room to his, as he changed his clothes. He babbled and bragged of his conquests. His conceit was unlimited, but she more than anyone loved to hear his chatter. She believed it all, because in her eyes he was so divinely handsome and had such adorable ways that she could not imagine how any woman could resist him. Her one terror was that one of them would be wily enough to capture him, now she was not there to protect him. She needn't have worried, for he was as crafty as a fox and more slippery than any eel, and while he could trade his looks for such handsome presents, he would be a fool to tie himself up to one woman. He had already decided quite definitely that the only reason he would have to get married would be if his financial resources failed. Then he would marry some wretched girl who had a handsome *dot*. He didn't see why he should work for a living: he didn't like work, he liked a good time. 'Good-time Charlie,' he said, swaggering about half-dressed.

Yes, money, that was the damnable stumbling-block. Not that he actually lacked any single thing that he wanted — his parents were really pretty generous to him, especially his mother — but somehow he was haunted by the most incredible bills, and they were always dunning him and threatening to tell his father.

Of course, if his father ever did hear about them, it would be goodnight. He was afraid of his father. Jacques was very strict with him: because he had a high moral sense himself, he thought everyone else should too. If he knew one-third of Raoul's nasty tricks he would have a fit and probably die of shame; Raoul was always very subdued and deferential in his father's presence.

His mother was altogether different; he could wind her round his little finger, or so he thought. Yet today, just when he was maddeningly short of money and was being hard-pressed, she was being unusually difficult. She wanted to know what he wanted the money for, and she plainly refused to believe his lies when he told her. She felt he had had quite enough money recently, and it would not hurt him to do without for a little. He sensed that for once he was not going to get it all his own way, and his slanting brown eyes smouldered with rage.

He knew he could get round her in time, but time was just what he lacked. Who else was there? Aunt Hattie? His brow creased as he sleeked back his golden hair. And where, pray, was that infernal girl Prudence? She should be back by now. It was too annoying. Everything was conspiring to frustrate him today . . . Or was it?

He stared at himself incredulously in the mirror, surprised at his own thoughts. Was this perhaps the very opportunity he needed? His brain clicked merrily from point to point. At last he shrugged and, slipping a silver cigarette case into his hip pocket, tiptoed to the doorway.

His mother appeared to be asleep.

He drew in his breath softly and moved across the room to the open bureau. With his eyes fixed watchfully on her immobile face, his fingers groped at the back of a pigeonhole, pressing and sliding. There was a faint click, and a panel swung outwards . . .

The eager fingers had found what they sought. He replaced the panel. With one hand hidden in his pocket he approached the high bed and stood staring down at the pale, still-handsome face with a strange, almost pitying expression.

But he did not linger there long, and in his haste to escape he left his mother's door ajar.

Julia's eyes were open and filled with fear. A convulsive tremor passed through her frame. She gave a horrible gurgling cry . . .

Raoul ran helter-skelter down the steps that led to Wigtown. He must not be late.

Where was that cursed girl?

★   ★   ★

The unlatched door opened impercepti-
bly to disclose an inquisitive black face. A
dust-coloured Siamese cat padded into
the room, sat down in the middle of the
floor, squinted her pale blue eyes
hideously, and began to wash her face.
Presently, with a whine she sprang onto
the bed . . .

2

La Morte

There were only two hotels in Wigtown:
the Royal Splendide and Simpson's
Family Hotel. Quentin Seal was fooled by
the name and chose the Royal Splendide,
but he had not been there long before he
realised his mistake. However, he did not
bother to move. He was not over-fussy
about fleas and dust. His motto was more
or less *Where I am, I lie*.

He had a lazy, easy-going temperament. Except that he liked to travel, he
never wanted to do things. It was
sufficient for him just to *be*; there was so
much to be experienced passively. He
liked people, too, and he enjoyed nothing
better than watching their idiosyncrasies
and satisfying his insatiable curiosity over
human relationships. His wants were
simple and could be satisfied anywhere.
His one expensive taste was travel, and

25

even that he was willing to do modestly — not so far as distance, but so far as mode, was concerned.

But even the cheapest kind of living requires money: the merest daily bread has to be earned. So Quentin Seal wrote detective stories for his livelihood. It was the quickest way he knew of making money that was not immoral. Two novels a year provided him with sufficient money to enable him to lead the kind of life he enjoyed, and they were really very little trouble to write. He had a logical mind and rather enjoyed inventing complicated puzzles. As for the actual writing of them: when the exchequer became uncomfortably low, he retired to some still place, barricaded himself in, wrote day and night in a perfect frenzy of energy, and would not allow himself to be disturbed until it was finished. Trays of food were placed outside his door and he brewed himself endless quantities of strong coffee. He slept in snatches till the whole business was over and he staggered out once more into the light of day, red-eyed, irritable, and bored, but looking forward to a long, delicious bout of freedom. This way, he managed to achieve about ten months' idleness a year, against a few weeks' excruciatingly hard work. He preferred it like that.

In spite of these methods, his books were surprisingly intelligent, and his reputation was high among the more sober and scholarly fans. It amused him to be greeted with something approaching veneration by some learned professor.

He lay panting now on the sagging wooden veranda facing the quiet street. It was brutally hot. The glaring sun had washed all colour from the sky. The white street quivering with heat was empty of bystanders. Although Seal had been only a few days in Wigtown, he knew that to be unusual; it was generally rowdy enough despite the weather. Unaware of the feast, he wondered where everyone had got to.

Oh, to be a fish in the uttermost depths of the icy sea where no ray of sun ever penetrated! A long iced drink was what he needed more than anything else; but ring as he might, no one answered his bell.

This so-called hotel appeared to be empty. He wondered uneasily whether everyone but he had had news of an impending earthquake or hurricane.

He plunged his head into a basin of coldish water, made himself look as respectable as he could, and decided to call on a certain French Creole — Monsieur Jacques, Premier Justice — to whom he had been given a letter of introduction. As a rule he refused these banal entries into polite society, but this one his mutual friend had promised would be interesting. He surveyed himself with disapproval in the fly-blown mirror His water-dark hair plastered back over his large skull, his broad humorous nose and wide mouth, and the way he had of lifting his slanting eyebrows, gave him a rather frog-like expression. He had a burly torso, and long slender legs, which carried out the frog effect.

He strolled out through the silent hotel into the glaring light of the dusty road. He woke up a sleeping beggar to inquire the whereabouts of Castelnuovo. The beggar had never heard of it, for it was always known as *Jacques'* or *Jacques' house*.

The castle walls and ancient creeper-clad tower were indubitably attractive, but Mr. Seal stared horror-struck at the steps stretching endlessly above him into the sky itself — a veritable Jacob's ladder! He might have turned back had it not been for the cold and sparkling drink dancing before his inward eye. A youth rushed down past him, apparently without even seeing him. Every few steps, he had to stop and rest on the stone balustrade. It was going to take a long time to reach the top.

When he finally reached the top he was rewarded by the splendid vista. The steps slackened into broad terraces running round the upper part of the house to the squat tower. The lower flat had the walled-in garden of the courtyard; the steps that led to it branched off from the others. He had missed the turn and had mounted, quite correctly as it happened, to the upper terrace. He leant against the massive wall, while the faintest little breeze flattered his brow. Below him,

Wigtown lay like a miniature town in a glass paperweight. It was deliciously peaceful — and astonishingly quiet. He very much hoped that they were not all out also. He turned to the door and tugged at the bell, listening to its reverberating and hollow echoes. No one came.

He moved away disconsolately, walking along the terrace and peering in at the windows . . .

Thus Mr. Seal was the first person to discover La Morte.

There was something uncanny, beastly, in the idea of a dead woman lying in an otherwise empty house, he thought, as he ran from room to room seeking some other inhabitant, seeking help. What *did* one do when one entered a strange house for the first time and found it solely inhabited by a corpse? It certainly put one in an invidious position. He ought, of course, to send for the doctor. But who was the doctor and where did he live? How to get in touch with him?

He discovered the lower part of the house and presently the way down to it also. Perhaps someone would be there.

A striped curtain hung over the open doorway and he pushed it aside. It smelt like a zoo, he thought, standing in the dim hall. As he grew accustomed to the dark, he perceived dirt, untidiness, horrid little saucers of food lying about the floor, and cats . . . cats everywhere.

All the doors led from one room to another. He was on the point of deciding that no one was there, when he saw in the shadowy corner of a large tawdry room a huge woman stretched flat on her back on a divan. There was something so hideously abandoned in her attitude that his heart lurched suddenly.

There surely couldn't be *two* women . . . He moved forward.

A harsh scream brought him to a standstill again. He turned sharply, to see a little grey gibbon swing itself down from the curtain-rail, chattering angrily. At the same instant the woman on the divan gave a tremendous snort and sat up. She held out her arms and the gibbon rushed to their shelter, expostulating shrilly.

'That jumped me out of ten years'

growth,' complained Quentin, with a disarming smile.

The woman stared blankly. 'And who the devil may you be?'

'I'm a stranger to you. My excuse for intruding on you is a matter of life and death.'

'Fancy!' she cooed, stroking the monkey's fur. 'You hear that, my pretty? Isn't that thrilling!'

'Chiefly death.'

'Oh, dear, we *do* hope the gentleman hasn't come all this way to try and interest us in insurance!'

He was revolted by her maudlin inanity.

'I'd be glad if you could tell me how to get hold of a doctor, madam. There's a woman lying upstairs, dead!'

To his amazement, she cackled uproariously and kissed her pet's black velvet face.

'Did you hear that, my precious? Tee hee!' She turned to him. 'That's my poor sister,' she explained. 'She isn't dead. She's paralysed. Helpless from head to foot.'

'I am sorry I was so abrupt about it, then, but I couldn't guess she was your sister. I'm afraid there is no mistake about it — she *is* dead.'

'Dead!' she said incredulously. 'Julia dead!' She lumped her legs over the edge of the divan and pulled herself upright. The bright colour had left her face and it was mottled a suety-white, with two hard chips of turquoise for eyes. Her whole personality seemed to have changed in a twinkling. She shook the monkey off her shoulder.

'We'd better go and see what's to be done,' she said quietly.

The nurse was there when they got back, feeling rather uneasy. Whilst she was entitled to her time off, it did look so unprofessional to have the patient die with no one on duty. She hoped the doctor would not blame her. She had always done her best for the poor woman. Anyway, there was no point in sentimentality: it was a blessed release. Of course, one couldn't possibly say so. It had worked out nicely for her, anyway; for she had been there just over two years, and was bored to tears with the job, and heartily sick of Apostle. She wondered where Miss Whitaker was. The doctor would want to hear the details of the death.

The doctor did not blame anyone. He was not so very surprised at the sudden demise, for, although he could not pretend that he actually expected it just then, it had been an unpredictable illness from the start, and it was quite on the cards that she might one day have another attack which would prove fatal. It really was impossible to forecast in these matters. It was always awkward for the poor practitioner. He was supposed to be infallible, but if he wasn't, they said he was no good and lost faith in him. If he told them the patient might die at any moment, they fidgeted and fretted; but if he said there was no danger and then the patient died, they were furious at not having been warned. Oh, well!

It would be interesting to have a post-mortem, but the family always made a fuss about that sort of thing. And it was hardly necessary, really; there was no doubt in his mind that she had succumbed to another stroke. He asked who was with her when she died.

There was a little silence.

Mr. Seal coughed: 'I — er — found her. There was no one with her.'

'I don't understand.' The doctor frowned. 'She was never left for more than a few moments together. She was quite helpless, you know; if she had wanted anything ... How was it you weren't there, Nurse?'

'It was my free time, Doctor. There was some shopping I had to do in Wigtown. I arranged that Miss Whitaker should stay with her.'

'Miss Whitaker?'

'My secretary,' explained Miss Brown. 'A mousy little thing; I'm not surprised you never noticed her. If I had nothing particular for her to do, I never minded her coming up here to sit with my sister. In fact, I was quite glad for poor Julia to have a little change of society. She used to quite look forward to Nurse's days off, I believe.' She darted a glance in the nurse's direction.

'Yes, yes. But where is Miss Whitaker?'

Hattie looked about her vaguely.

'Who knows? Very likely she lost her head and bolted, pretending to herself that she was going to get help. Silly little fool!'

'If she had wanted help, surely you were the nearest person?'

She shrugged.

'I don't think it can have been quite like that,' remarked Mr. Seal. 'Miss Whitaker must have gone before the lady died.'

'What makes you think so?'

'I'm pretty certain she didn't die from natural causes. She was suffocated.' He watched their faces curiously. Miss Brown pulled at the neck of her dress as if she were choking.

'Suffocated! How do you know?'

'I saw it.'

Prudence Whitaker stood swaying in the doorway, the rims of her glasses dark against her paper-white face. 'Who?' she gasped.

'I meant to say that I saw the marks of it. You will observe on her face, Doctor, scratches — there, by her cheek — and under her chin. You see?'

'Well?' said the doctor sharply.

'Were they there before?' He turned to the nurse. She shook her head doubtfully. 'I thought not. They looked quite fresh and angry to me. Very well, how did they come there?'

Hattie said irritably: 'I don't care for the tone of your insinuations, Mr. — er — '

'Seal. Quentin Seal,' he said,

'If you imagine it was in the slightest interest of anyone to harm my poor sister, you are quite mistaken, Mr. Seal.'

'And anyway, you feel it is none of my business.' He smiled coolly. 'I just thought I ought to mention it to the doctor. It is such a mistake, or so I have always found, not to mention any curious little factor or discrepancy that strikes one at the time. It nearly always comes out sooner or later, and then it causes such a lot of needless misery. If you want to hush the whole thing up, it is much better for everyone to know clearly where they stand in the matter, then there are no uncomfortable surprises or useless recriminations.'

'Mr. Seal evidently speaks from a wide experience. However, we mustn't take advantage of his broadmindedness. I'm sure the doctor will advise us what to do.'

'Or Mr. Jacques,' interpolated Prudence quietly.

'Antoine!' cried the old woman, and clapped her hands to her cheeks in dismay. 'I'd quite forgotten. We must let him know at once. What's the time?'

'He'll be back from the courts directly,' said somebody. 'Poor man, whatever will he do?'

He entered, as if on a cue.

Antoine Jacques was in his fifties, reserved and inclined to pessimism, perhaps because of his bad health. He was still handsome, despite his sallow complexion and dark-ringed weary eyes. With his elegantly greying hair, he looked like a slightly debilitated Spanish grandee. It was easy to imagine that in his youth he must have been irresistible to a certain type of woman.

He stared at them all now, silently and with a dawning horror.

'*Bon Dieu!*' he said. 'Something has happened to Julia . . . Tell me quickly . . . She's dead! Is that it?' His face became livid and he spread out his hands blindly as if seeking support. Hattie rushed to his side.

'Oh, darling! It's terrible, but she didn't suffer, Antoine, it was very quick. Oh, my poor dear, don't look like that. We must console one another. I've lost a sister, too, you know.' She began to cry.

He pushed her away, not unkindly, but as if he did not know who she was. He walked unsteadily over to the bed.

'I would like to be left alone with her for just a few minutes,' he said.

In the other room, Hattie pulled herself together and offered them all much-needed drinks. They partook in gloomy silence.

'We have not yet had Miss Whitaker's account of the affair,' the doctor suggested drily.

Prudence moistened her pale lips nervously.

'Of course it was very wrong of me. I won't attempt to excuse myself. There

were some things I had to do ...
registered letters ... and that sort of
thing ... in Wigtown. I didn't mean to
be long. Oh, I didn't leave her alone.
Don't think that. Raoul promised to
stay with her till I got back. I don't
know what has become of him ... I
thought it would be all right,' she added
helplessly.

Well, then, where on earth was Raoul?
It certainly seemed a little odd the way
everybody had chosen this day of all days
to rely on someone else to stay with the
invalid; each person in turn had slipped
away from the post of duty, almost as
though the whole thing had been
carefully prearranged ...

Raoul, very beautiful in his immaculate
white flannels, came lightly towards the
little group.

Hattie stepped towards him accusingly.

'Where *have* you been, you wicked boy?
What have you been up to?'

The boy took a nervous step backwards
and looked at them uncertainly.

'Why, Auntie, what's the matter? Is
anything wrong?'

'What *should* be wrong?' she said sharply.

'I don't know — I didn't mean anything. My goodness! Only you are all looking so — '

'I'm afraid we have got rather bad news for you,' said the doctor kindly. 'Your dear mother — you must be prepared — '

'Mater!' cried Raoul. 'What has happened to her? My God, she's not — ' The word stuck in his throat. He put his hands over his face. And then, as if he could no longer bear their eyes on him another instant, pushed roughly past them into the inner room. He paused for an instant on the threshold of his mother's room, and then he hurled himself on his knees by her bed and burst into a flood of tears.

Jacques, who deplored any demonstration of emotion, was repelled by his son's unrepressed howling. He winced, but waited patiently for the sobbing to subside. When it showed no signs of doing so, Jacques touched him on the shoulder gently, speaking to him — as usual — in French.

'Come, my child,' he said. 'You'll do

yourself no good by this.'

'Oh, Papa, Papa,' he blubbered in a frenzy. 'It was all my fault. I killed her. What shall I do?'

'Calm yourself, my boy.'

He sprang to his feet, and grasped his father's coat.

'I tell you, I killed her!' he shrieked. 'Don't you understand? It was my fault.'

'Go to your room, Raoul. You are hysterical.'

'Just a minute, Antoine, if you please,' Hattie interrupted. 'I should like to ask Raoul where he has been all this while. Miss Whitaker says that she left him here while she went out for a minute . . . '

'She never came back,' Raoul gulped. 'I told her I couldn't wait long, that I had an important engagement. At last I couldn't wait any longer. I thought she was bound to be back soon . . . '

'I was longer than I meant to be,' admitted Prudence dolefully.

'It must have been a very important engagement for you to leave your mother alone — to die,' said Hattie cruelly.

'How was I to know?' he wailed.

Of course, it had all to be explained to Jacques. It certainly sounded a bad business, told baldly like that. And when it came to the marks on the dead woman's face . . .

The doctor would have liked to pooh-pooh the idea of foul play that was buzzing in some of their minds, but it was not his place to do more than give it as his considered opinion that she had died of muscular paralysis following a secondary stroke.

On the other hand, it was scarcely possible for a man in Jacques' position just to let the whole thing slide as though it were of no importance. If there was the slightest doubt in anyone's mind, it was his duty to uphold the law and see that all was done that could possibly be done to clear the matter up satisfactorily. It would mean an inquest.

And an inquest, the doctor reminded him, meant a post-mortem.

What finally decided the matter was the discovery that Julia's desk had been tampered with. She kept her money in a purse in a secret drawer, and it was gone:

two thousand francs of it. Who could have taken it? The money had only been put there the day before. The most likely suspects were the servants, of course, particularly in view of the feast day with all its possibilities for spending. But then, when could they have taken it? They could neither have taken it when anyone else was there, nor when she was awake — or alive — to see them. There was just a remote chance that one of them had come back to the house, found her alone and yielded to the temptation. No, even that was beyond the bounds of possibility, for there were only two or three people who knew where her money was kept, and they were not the servants.

That narrowed it down to the last people who were known to have seen her. Hattie was unlikely, because although she knew of the secret panel, she had plenty of money of her own, and also the priest had come in before she left. Father Xavier, on the other hand, had come out to fetch the nurse, so he had had the opportunity. But did he know where the money was kept? There was no knowing what the dead woman had confided to him. And though he always desperately needed money for his parish, one could hardly imagine him sinking to such formidable depths to acquire it. Prudence was out of it, because she had not come up after all. That left Raoul and the nurse.

'But of course I didn't take it,' said Raoul, wide-eyed. 'Why ever should I? I have all the money I need. And if there is anything special I want to buy, Mater always lets me have the money. I only have — had — to ask.'

The nurse flushed a bright red.

'If you think I took it, send for the police and have my bags searched, while you're about it! I'm not accustomed to being accused of theft, and I don't like it.'

'No one has accused you yet, Nurse,' said Mr. Seal quietly. 'There is a far more likely suspect whom they have not yet mentioned.' He looked round at them with a little smile.

'*I* was up here alone with the deceased, don't forget, and no one knows for quite how long, either. I may have had plenty of time to nimble around to see what I could pick up. Of course I didn't, but you've only my word for it.'

'That's all very fine, Mr. Seal, but I have my professional reputation to consider. Nice it would look for me to be accused of theft, wouldn't it? On top of all this other business, too. Not that *I* was the last person to see the dear soul. *I* did my duty all right; my conscience is quite clear on that point. *I* have nothing to reproach myself with. Still, it doesn't do for a nurse to be mixed up in anything unsavoury; it can do me a lot of harm.'

'Yes, Nurse, we see your point of view and we sympathise with you. But our one interest is to see that the ends of justice are served. I'm sure we all agree over that,' said Jacques wearily.

'Perhaps it would be best to leave it for now,' suggested Mr. Seal. 'If you want me for anything, I am to be found at the Royal Splendide.'

3

Funeral

The affair of the two thousand francs was not mentioned at the inquest. M. Donbas, solicitor, was the coroner, and he knew how to deal with these matters.

The nurse was calm and unflustered; she had done nothing out of her usual routine. Her patient had seemed no different from usual. Even though it was her due, she would never have left her patient, of course, if she had known that Miss Whitaker was not going to remain with her as she promised. But she was not to know that Miss Whitaker would fail her. It was not a new arrangement between them and had always proved perfectly satisfactory before. The only flaw in all this was that she had not remained until Miss Whitaker arrived on the scene.

Miss Whitaker's case was not quite so

good. She pleaded in extenuation that she had found a substitute in Raoul. Asked why she had not told the nurse that she had other things to do that afternoon, she mumbled that she had not remembered these particular chores until it was too late to let the nurse know.

There was some question of registering a letter, the coroner suggested tentatively. And, when she concurred, jumped down on her like a hawk for not remembering that the post office was closed that day on account of the feast. She *had* forgotten, she said; it was stupid of her, but it had gone clean out of her head until she arrived in front of its closed doors. M. Donbas sympathised rather ostentatiously with her remarkably poor memory. So it was all for nothing, her journey? Why, then, had she not returned at once? She had taken the autobus into Belleville, she confessed, and posted it from the post office there. Doubtless, Miss Whitaker had retained the registration receipt? Miss Whitaker, blushing, fumbled in her bag and finally produced it — to everyone's surprise.

Raoul did not come out so well, either. Mainly because he refused to say where he had gone. Although it was explained to him that his silence allowed them to put their own interpretation on the known facts, his lips remained gallantly but stubbornly sealed. Stupid little boy!

Mr. Seal, on the other hand, rather let himself go. He explained how it was that he was there to discover Madame Jacques; that he had found an open window and entered.

'Did you suspect that anything was wrong?' asked the coroner.

'I did. No one could be alive with a cat sitting on her head. It was obvious to the meanest intelligence that something was wrong. As I came in the cat sprang up, arching its back and spitting, and when I lifted it down it stretched out its claws defensively and scratched the dead woman's face. I quickly made sure that life was quite extinct and then went in search of help. It seemed pretty clear to me, in view of what I subsequently learnt about Madame Jacques' malady, that somehow or other the cat got into her room when there was no one there to protect her; and of course, once it had settled itself over her face, she would be powerless to move it.'

There was what they call a sensation in court. Jacques' face had a greenish pallor. Seal answered the rest of the questions without excitement. The nurse remembered seeing the priest bring a cat out of the room — remembered it scratching him, too. Father Xavier admitted it. He did not think the cat could have got back again directly afterwards, for he had shut the door. Unless, of course, the nurse had let it in accidentally and it had contrived to secrete itself under the bed or in a cupboard.

The coroner's jury condoled with the bereaved husband, and to a lesser degree with the son and the sister. They could not help intimating mildly that there seemed to have been some astonishing negligence somewhere. They entered a verdict of death by misadventure, for the blame could be fastened on no one person.

Nurse departed huffily. It was always the same with relatives. One devoted oneself to one's patient, and when he or she died, one was thrown out. Gratitude? That was only in the dictionary.

Once the inquest was behind them, they could devote their whole minds to the funeral — important affairs, these, on Apostle Island, the greatest of the three eternal mysteries: birth, marriage and death.

Everyone who was anyone was invited. Mr. Seal was among those present, of course. The residence was all incredibly altered to him — he could scarcely believe it was the same place. Previously it had seemed rather casual and ramshackle, a negligent air due partly to the absence of servants on that occasion. Now the keynote was solemn magnificence. Hattie had thought of everything, and created an air of ghoulish, baroque splendour.

From the stone archway leading to the courtyard hung an immense wreath of black feathers with scarlet ribbons drooping like bloody pennants. It struck a note of horror at once in its blackness and weird featheriness, an eerie warning of what would one day befall them all. A flag drooped limply at half-mast from the tower. The house itself stood square and white in the sun, its closed shutters proclaiming desolation. By way of contrast — and necessity — all the doors were open.

The meagre light that trickled through the pierced jalousies threw a darkly greenish tint over everything, giving it all a mysterious drowned appearance as though it were fathoms-deep beneath the sea.

Gusts of dizzying perfume were blown through the open doors from the ghostly flowers heaped bank-high: lilies, tuberoses, full white peonies, and the tall indigenous marguerites with surprising black centres and a peculiar numbing scent.

In the centre of the room lay La Morte, in an ebony coffin draped with white satin. The candles massed at her head and feet flickered uneasily in the draught.

The native servants in their mourning

liveries were as black as ravens, terrify-ingly black, as they padded discreetly to and fro. Featureless ghosts, Seal fancied them to be, more positive than shadows. For decency's sake, the cats had been confined somewhere safely, but now and again their shrill howling sounded like a banshee wail.

But Orlando, the gibbon, promenaded soberly about, clinging to his mistress's hand as she moved among the guests. With his neat grey fur and respectful black velvet face he looked like a seventeenth-century mourning dwarf.

People streamed in and out endlessly to pay their last respects to the dead woman: black, white, and yellow, bowing and chattering. Some were there from duty and some from love, but most of them were there out of curiosity and love of spectacle and the determination not to miss what might be one of the biggest parties of the year. There was all the solemn splendour to keep you a-shiver . . . and the 'eats and licker', followed by the good time, which was mysteriously heightened by the knowledge that one of the number was missing, while you were still one of the lucky ones left behind to drink and eat and sin and dance and make love. Death, playing tag, hadn't caught you.

When the candles had worn down in their sockets they came to fetch La Morte away. Seal watched the black and silver pall lurching away down the steps, smaller and smaller, to the thumbnail hearse below. The dark procession followed it. The sun discreetly drew a handkerchief of mist to its face, but that did nothing to lessen the vaporous heat. Even the trees appeared to be wilting, their broad leaves yellowing and drooping. Now and again the palm-trees shivered as the melancholy procession passed, and with frightened squawks birds fled from the track.

Father Xavier read the last service. The queer damp smell of hot earth rose up to them as they entered the churchyard. Amid an awful silence the coffin was lowered to its clammy grave; and with a sudden outburst of cries and groans, flowers were tossed, torn and ragged, in a pelting mass on to the coffin lid until it was completely covered.

Then everyone trooped back to the house, the priest with them. In their absence all had been prepared: shutters flung back, candles extinguished, long tables laden with food. And they were ready for it, too. There was nothing like emotion to give one an appetite.

Hattie introduced John Foley, the bailiff of her estate, to Quentin Seal. He was the hearty type of Englishman with doggy eyes.

'Out from England, eh? Lucky chap! What part?'

'Putney,' said Quentin, who had no false pride.

'Putney!' he said wistfully. 'What wouldn't I give to be there now? My God, that spells romance to me — Putney! I dream of it; Putney on a damned awful raw November day when you can't see your hand in front of your face. It's still the same, I suppose. You must come to our place for a meal and tell us all about it. Where are you staying? The Royal Splendide? You poor devil! Eve calls it the place where beachcombers go to die. You must meet my wife. Good lord, fancy missing primroses in an English lane, and village cricket, and all the fine fellows at the golf club in order to stay at the Royal Splendide in Wigtown! Still, I suppose it's not *too* bad if you know that you don't have to stay . . . Oh, Eve, this is Mr. — er — Seal.'

Evelyn Foley was in her late thirties; attractive, if you liked them coldly sensual. She had a dead-white skin and a mouth like a drooping scarlet flower that just asked to be petted into good humour. Heavy contemptuous lids veiled her green eyes. She seemed to flaunt her sensuality with a studied insolence. She was very sure of herself. Her hand in his was cool and inquiring.

Film vamp of 1920, thought Quentin in self-defence.

She smiled at him sardonically, as if she had read his thoughts. Without removing her hand or withdrawing her eyes from his, she spoke to her husband:

'John, Mr. Seal hasn't got anything to drink. I'm sure he's longing for one: I know I am. Bring two, darling. We'll be on the terrace ... ' She sauntered through the crowd, smart in her shiny black straw hat and austere little black frock, only relieved by a pair of diamond and emerald clips at the neckline.

The sea was a hard, smooth, transparent jade, and the sky above faded almost white with heat. It was restful and pleasant outside after the cacophonous chatter within.

'The exotic always seems a trifle sinister to me,' murmured Seal.

'You don't mean that personally, I suppose?' She smiled languorously. 'If you mean this place, I couldn't agree with you more. I'm frankly terrified of it. I hate it. I wish to God I could get away from it. I know if I don't, it'll get me one day. It gets everyone in the end. It's cruel, devilish ... You think I'm fanciful? It's the truth. Look what it did to Julia Jacques! It's no place for white people, I tell you. It got my little baby, and it won't be satisfied till it gets me, too.' She put her hand to her throat. 'I'm sorry,' she said. 'Can I have a cigarette?'

He lit her one and she steadied his

hand with her white fingers. She expelled the smoke in a long grey plume. 'Forgive me for being so silly and dramatic, please. It's my nerves . . . And all this . . . I was rather fond of poor Julia. Besides, you're so sympathetic. I can never talk about it to Johnny, you see. It wouldn't be fair; the poor old boy has enough to bear as it is. But sometimes it makes me feel hideously lonely. I miss my little baby so dreadfully — too many memories here. And, you see, I can never have another child now. That's what makes me so bitter . . . ' Tears glittered charmingly on her long lashes.

'Here we are again!' cried Foley cheerfully. 'I brought Long Gins. Hope that's all right. Cheers!'

'Well, you didn't have a very auspicious beginning to your stay, Mr. Seal. What an unpleasant business it has been, and then the inquest and all that. Horrible!' Evelyn shuddered.

'Dashed awkward business, breaking it to the family, too,' said Foley. 'Shouldn't like that myself.'

'Still, it's an ill wind that blows nobody

any good,' said Evelyn, swirling a lump of ice around her empty glass.

'Now then, old girl, what are you getting at?' Foley chuckled slyly.

'I'm not insinuating that it was in someone's interest to be rid of her. Don't be an ass, Johnny. I merely meant that Jacques will be glad to be free again — once he has got over the first grief . . . No, I'm not being a cat. It stands to reason that to be tied to a hopeless invalid is enough to get on anyone's nerves.'

'Nonsense, Eve, he's always been devoted to her.'

'Mr. Seal knows what I mean.'

Raoul came toward them, dramatic in his funeral garb. He saw they had noticed him, and stopped. 'Madame!'

He bowed and kissed her hand mournfully without looking at her. He shook hands with Gallic intensity with the two men. There was an awkward halt in the conversation.

'Haven't seen you over at our place for some time, Raoul. Why don't you come over anymore, eh? Drop in any time, you're always welcome, you know. Come over to a meal — well, you can't very well tonight, but how about tomorrow? Cheer you up.'

'No, Johnny darling, that wouldn't do at all. You embarrass the poor boy. Naturally, he doesn't want to go out visiting when he's just lost his mother. Later on, we'll be delighted to see him,' said Eve gently, fingering her jewelled clips. 'Men are so insensitive sometimes,' she remarked at large.

'He doesn't want to brood, my dear. He's young; he wants to be taken out of himself a little. All this, now — ' He waved a hand. ' — it gives me the creeps. Nothing but morbid extravagance. And what's the good of it, eh? Who benefits?'

Yes, thought Quentin, *that is just the point — who benefits?*

'Well, I hope when it's my turn they'll bury me at sea,' said Foley. 'Can't stand fuss. I dare say it's different for you; you're half-foreign, anyway. But you don't want to give way to it.' Though whether it was foreignness or morbidity that he should not give way to was not quite clear. And if Raoul was mentally thumbing his nose at Foley, you would never have guessed it from the courtly grace with which he acknowledged his advice.

The guests were beginning to take their leave. The sun was sliding down the sky. Evelyn, suddenly bored, plucked at Foley's arm for him to take her away.

'Be sure to come over and see us,' she called back to Quentin. But she drifted away without even remembering to say goodbye to the young Jacques.

He bowed low to her retreating back. 'Charmed!' he said sarcastically under his breath. And to Seal, politely: 'May I get you something to drink, sir?'

'I'll come with you.' They strolled off side by side. 'People are queer, aren't they? They both apparently hate this place like poison, so why do they stay? Surely he could get a job in England. Or is he wanted by the police, do you suppose?'

'Very possible, I should think. But I do not think they really hate it here. They just talk that way. Everybody does. It's chic.'

'A quaint custom. It fooled me,

anyway. He really did sound awfully homesick. And I could appreciate that she would hate the place after losing her baby — '

'Losing her *what*?' shrieked Raoul. 'Oh, I shall kill myself with laughing!' he exclaimed mirthlessly. '*Mon Dieu*, and you believed her! She has never had a baby, not ever.'

'Why on earth should she pretend to me that she had, then? And lost it so tragically?'

'Oh, to make herself interesting, no doubt, to an attractive stranger . . . '

Prudence had retired to her room with a cracking headache, so she said, and asked to be let alone. But as soon as the guests had thinned out, Hattie came scrabbling at the door and rattling at the handle.

'Miss Whitaker, are you asleep?'

Fat chance, thought Miss Whitaker sulkily, as she slid off the bed to unlock the door.

'Oh, you were lying down! I'm so sorry to have disturbed you. Get back on the bed again,' she said, insincerely and petulantly. 'I only thought you might have helped me a little with all the guests; it's been such a lot for me to see to alone. But it doesn't matter now, you needn't bother yourself, because most of them have gone.'

'I'm awfully sorry, Miss Brown,' said Prudence meekly. 'But honestly, I could hardly stand up, my head was so bad.'

'I expect a lot of it is due to panic. It can't be very nice to know that everyone is holding you morally responsible for my sister's death — eyes staring at you, and muttering from mouth to mouth as you pass. Still, by rights that should make you more eager than ever not to shirk your duty again, shouldn't it . . . ? No, no, there's no need to be foolish. Let them think what they like. It's too late now.'

'If you feel like that about it, perhaps you would rather I gave you my notice,' mumbled Miss Whitaker.

'Don't be a silly girl. You're over-wrought. Lie down and I'll send you to sleep, and when you wake up you'll have forgotten all about it.' Her heavy paw began sliding down the girl's arm with long steady strokes. 'Do you like that?'

'As a matter of fact, if you won't think me rude, Miss Brown, I can't stand being touched.' Her flesh really shrank from it.

'Never mind. In a little while you'll like it. It'll soothe you, and the rhythm will send you to sleep. I've got a magical touch — healing hands that send great currents of vitality from me to you. It's a hereditary gift. My grandmother had it. They used to say she was a vampire, you know. She killed two husbands, her housekeeper, and goodness knows how many other people . . . villagers, who disappeared without a trace, so it is said. It's a subject that fascinates me . . . I'm supposed to be very like my grandmother. I think I've inherited her spirit.' She leant her great face with its light staring eyes close to the girl's. 'Do you believe in vampires?'

With a tremendous effort Prudence laughed. 'Good heavens, no. I'm afraid I'm not at all imaginative, Miss Brown; too mundane.' It was a brave attempt, for Miss Brown terrified her in these moods, and she longed to scream and push her away.

The dying sun sank into the flaming sea, its blood streaking the primrose sky. In a few minutes it would be dark . . .

The priest and the doctor lingered on the terrace, beneath the welcome shade of the big lime tree.

'Where have all the family got to? I have not noticed them around for quite a while.'

'I saw M. Donbas come up a short while ago,' said the little priest. 'So I should not be surprised if he has come to discuss the will, or something of that nature.'

'Donbas, eh? Good lord! I hope it is only the will that's fetched him up.'

'What else should it be, my friend?'

'I don't know . . . They say confession is good for the soul, Father. And you must be pretty used to it by now. I've got rather a guilty conscience, I'm afraid, about the inquest. I behaved really very stupidly. It is always so much wiser to tell the truth, but it seemed easier to concur with the accepted opinion. You see,

Madame Jacques was dead before the cat stifled her. My original diagnosis was correct: Madame Jacques died of a secondary stroke.'

'The devil she did! How do you make that out?'

'Listen; you knew her as well as I did. She was perfectly capable of making *some* effort. She could have — shall we say — bitten the animal to make it move. But she didn't. And not only that, not one trace of fur, not a single cat hair was found in her nose, throat, or lungs — that proves she must have been dead already.'

'I suppose it does — '

From out the French windows sped a slim black figure towards them.

'Villain! What have you done? You have ruined us all!' He seized the priest by the shoulders and shook him violently, his face distorted with rage.

'Raoul!' said the doctor sharply, and pulled him away. 'Have you gone off your head?'

'It would be no wonder if I had,' snarled the boy. 'This creeping swine! I'll have the law on him. I'll get my own back, see if I don't. The rat! The traitor!'

'My dear boy, I beg you — ' murmured the priest.

'Do you want to know what he has done? He's taken advantage of his position of trust to worm his way into my poor Mater's confidence, and he has influenced her — influenced her,' he repeated, choking over the words, 'to leave all her money to him. I, her only son, have got nothing. Is that right? Is it just? I appeal to you, *Monsieur le Docteur*, is it even sane?'

'There's nothing specifically insane in willing one's money to whom one pleases. She was not compelled to leave it to you; the law does not require it. She very likely thought you had sufficient.'

'But I haven't *anything*,' he cried impatiently, almost tearing his hair out. 'I'm penniless. Either I must be dependent on Papa, or I must *work*,' he said, in the tones of one doomed to a leper colony.

'Well, it might even do you good.' The doctor could not help smiling.

'Good! While *my* money is squandered

on the Church . . . altar candles or a gold monstrance . . . or some such bloody rot, I suppose. That is, if he means to spend any of it on the Church — which I very much doubt. I don't suppose the slimy beast will waste any of it on the natives. Why should he?'

'I must say, I don't think you're behaving at all well over it.'

'You would side with him! Theology and Medicine, the world's greatest charlatans, hand in hand. Do you think *he* has behaved well to me? My God, I'd like to kill him! If I could just get my hands round his filthy neck!'

'Raoul!' came a sharp cry from the darkness. 'Cease, that at once. You should be ashamed to behave so — today of all days. I am shocked at your indecency. You will apologise immediately and then you will go to your room and remain there until further notice.'

But for once Raoul did not fear his father.

'Not damn likely, Papa! You don't know what you ask . . . That I should apologise to that black bastard — '

Jacques' hand smacked him hard across the face, so that he reeled and almost lost his balance.

'Go!' commanded Jacques in an icy dispassionate voice.

'On my son's behalf, I apologise most humbly to you, Father. It would be charitable to suppose that grief has momentarily unhinged his brain.'

The boy backed away, sobbing with rage, and hurling vituperations at them all in French.

'I am truly sorry,' said the priest, 'that it should happen so. He is so young and so wrapped in materialism that he can see nothing beyond it. Later he will understand. Then he will forgive even as he would wish to be forgiven.'

'It's easy enough to rattle off those pious remarks when you've got the dibs, Father,' said Hattie, in her high, malicious voice . . . They jumped uneasily. They had not heard her come up with her light, slurring tread.

'Antoine, you're too hard on the boy. He's only a child, and it's been a great blow to him. He can't believe that his own beloved mother would intentionally have left her money to a stranger and left him penniless. It's beyond belief, don't you see? He feels, naturally, that some kind of pressure or influence — '

'In the first place,' cut in Jacques, 'nothing on God's earth gives him the excuse to insult a guest. That is unforgivable. Also, he is not penniless while he is still under age and he has me to look after him. Moreover, he had no reason to assume that, in different circumstances, Julia would have left the money to her son rather than to her husband. The whole thing has been fabricated out of his angry imagination. I hope you will do your best not to encourage him in these absurd ideas, Hattie.'

'And I would like to add,' put in Father Xavier quietly, 'that the money was not left to a stranger, but to the Holy Church of God. If we could get away from this personal aspect of things, it would be so helpful. The money is of no use to me . . . It is for the greater glory of God . . . '

Hattie clapped sarcastic approval.

Mr. Seal, smoking on the terrace above them, watched the little group disperse.

Inside the house the lamps were being lit. Hattie and Jacques escorted the two men to the archway and watched them descend the steps until the darkness hid them.

Hattie stretched up her arm and pulled at the black feathers in the wreath, letting them flutter out of her fingers about the two of them, like sombre, autumnal confetti.

'Antoine, are you angry with old Hattie?' she said huskily. She put a hand on his sleeve. 'It was naughty of me, I know. But I simply can't stick that man. I know just how Raoul feels. You mustn't be cross with me. We've both lost the dearest person in the world — '

'Oh, please,' said Jacques wearily. 'Let's forget it. There isn't anything to forgive, is there? Good night, Hattie. Thank you for all you've done today.'

He climbed up the steps like an old man, put his hands out to open the French windows and then leant his head against the glass and let the tears roll

71

down his cheeks at last.

'Julia! Julia!' he murmured brokenly. 'What was it all for . . . ? How am I to carry on now . . . ?' He became aware that someone was watching him. He could just discern someone reflected darkly on the pane. He straightened up, self-disgusted. But, by the time he had brushed away all traces of his humiliating tears, whoever it was had gone.

4

Interlude

On Sundays, Miss Whitaker's time was her own. There was a rather nice little lagoon she had discovered with a beach of silvery sand, a mile or so beyond Wigtown, where she liked to bathe sometimes. It was so solitary that one could bathe in one's skin, a delicious sensuous indulgence of hers.

But on this occasion she found that someone had got there before her. She halted in dismay. From where she stood, it was impossible to tell whether it was a native or white person. The figure merged unrecognizably into the general nondescript background of sand and rock.

She came up close enough to see that the usurper was a white man, lying prone and motionless, wearing a ragged singlet and shabby near-white ducks. A battered native straw hat concealed his head and shoulders from sun and sight. On his feet he wore a primitive type of sandal of roughly woven palm-leaves.

Something in his pose made her catch her breath. Surely he was uncannily still. She moved nearer, but he did not stir at the sound of her crunching footsteps. Gingerly, she prodded him with the tip of her shoe: he maintained his supine posture. So, if he were dead, he was not yet cold and stiff. There might yet be time to revive him.

Summoning her courage, she knelt down beside him and removed his hat. His head was bald, polished mahogany by sun and wind. His face was buried in the crook of his arms. With an effort she grasped his warm shoulder and, gritting her teeth, pulled him up a little way from the ground. He rolled over on his back, unexpectedly. His lids flew back, disclosing large, drooping grey eyes. He was younger than his bald head had led her to expect. They gazed at one another in wordless astonishment.

'I — I beg your pardon,' she said, blushing.

'But not at all,' he smiled, propping himself on one elbow.

'I'm sorry I woke you up. I — I thought for a minute you were dead,' she explained with a nervous laugh.

'I'm glad. It is too long since I have been woken up by so beeyootiful a lady. Or one so brave, if you thought I was dead.' He spoke English with an unusual accent, his voice curiously deep. She could hardly understand him. And yet he was a white man. Prudence frowned fastidiously.

'It was more annoyance than courage, really. I'm afraid I've selfishly come to regard this little beach as my private property, and the thought of anyone else daring to monopolise it put my back up.'

But he did not take the broad hint. Instead, he stared at her hungrily in a way that would have embarrassed her if it had not been so unselfconscious. He had a big round head, and his eyes — so light in his chestnut face — set oddly wide apart and drooping at the outer corners, gave him an expression of ironical melancholy.

'Have you a cigarette you could spare

me?' he asked at last. She had, and gave him one. He consumed nearly half of it in one deep pull.

'There!' he said gaily. 'Twice you have saved my life in five minutes. It should be the other way round, but with English people it is never as one expects.'

She frowned her incomprehension.

'I don't speak good English?'

'Oh, yes. But I can't make out half you say. You speak like a bear talking to itself.'

'Ah, this is going to be a wonderful day,' he chuckled. 'To meet a lady beautiful, kind, brave, and also witty!'

'I must go,' she said abruptly, instinctively mistrusting complimentary strangers. She knew she was neither beautiful nor witty, and by no means always brave and kind.

'Don't leave!' he cried. 'Remain, if not for my sake, for the sake of your favourite beach.'

'It was the privacy that particularly appealed to me,' she said coldly.

'Ah, in that case — ' He lay back and there was nothing for her to do but walk away, impotently furious.

76

'Thank you for the cigarette,' he called.

She pretended not to hear. She was angry and hot and now there was no chance of a bathe. Her day was ruined. He was still calling after her, but she refused to turn round. At length she heard his footsteps padding behind her, and quickened her pace. He was closing up on her. Unexpectedly, fear split through her like forked lightning. She had never seen him before, but he might know very well who she was. Anything might happen . . . a lonely beach . . . no one within sight or sound . . . He could easily knock her down and drag her out to sea . . . If she were ever washed up: *Death by misadventure* — or, suicide — or anything. No one would ever know the truth . . .

Now right behind her, his hand gripped her wrist fiercely. White-lipped, she swung round to face him, ready to scream.

'If you are really going,' he rumbled, and pulled gently at the object she was grasping unconsciously in her hand, 'may I have my hat back, please?'

★　★　★

Of course she saw him again ... frequently. He never would talk much about himself, but by piecing together the fragments he dropped here and there, she managed to get a picture of his strange adventurous life. His name was Boris Borodin, and he was a White Russian from the Ukraine. What remained of his family were still there; he alone had escaped after the revolution.

Once, when he was describing to her the fighting in the early days of the war, she protested that he was too young to have seen it. Grinning, he explained that he had joined up with his father's regiment at the age of thirteen. He had run away once before when he was twelve and a half, and his father, the colonel, had whipped him and sent him home. The second time he ran away, he laughed and let him stay. For three years they led a wild and wonderful life. Then came the revolution, and the whole character of the fighting changed. He and his father were captured by the Reds. In those days, prisoners were shot. The Reds made them undress. Clothes were more precious than lives, then. He would always remember that day; the spring thaw had not yet set in and the snow was still thick-packed. It was very cold without clothes, like plunging into icy water. The soldiers told them to walk straight ahead. The young lad begged his father to go first, for he did not wish him to see his son killed. They shot the colonel in the back of the head, and he dropped like a stone. They wasted nothing in those days, not even bullets. The boy walked past his father's dead body, on and on, waiting for the shot that never came. Over the brow of the hill and out of sight, naked but free . . .

Soon after that he escaped from Russia altogether, and became a penniless wanderer on the face of the earth. Harbin . . . Shanghai . . . Vienna . . . Paris . . . Monte Carlo . . . Majorca . . . following the well-worn refugee track. Dishwasher, taxi-driver, barman, waiter, commission-aire — an endless list; and other jobs too, that were less polite but paid better money. There was nothing he was ashamed to try. He had courage, but not pride. Nor shame, either. He was quite content to beachcomb the Island, smooching about from hand to mouth, doing an odd job when actual starvation seemed imminent. Any feeble cravings for respectability and security had died long since; the adventurous freedom of vagrancy had him in thrall.

It was a queer friendship between the two of them. Prudence was shocked: as a man, and a healthy one, he ought to make some effort to climb above a life haunted by identity papers and hunger. It was Russian fatalism, she supposed. She grew to feel sorry for him; she helped him as much as she could; he became her foundling. In some odd way, it comforted her own loneliness and fear to have someone worse off than herself to look after.

And Boris was fascinated by her. It was years since he had been friendly with a woman of his own class, and in the far-off days when he had traded in his youth, the fine ladies who petted him also treated him with a veiled contempt. Now, although Prudence pretended to disapprove of him, he sensed she secretly rather admired him, and that was balm to his soul. He enjoyed shocking her and was endlessly amused at her innocence. Behind her wistful frailty he divined a great strength. He was fascinated by her, and more in love with her than he allowed himself to guess. She was astonished to find that though she commended honesty above all things, she would have preferred him to have hypocritically pretended he adored her madly and could not live without her. That he didn't even want her enough to put on an act for her seemed rather humiliating — or at least it would have been if she had looked on him as anything other than a poor wretch whom she was befriending out of the goodness of her heart.

But it was an unpleasant shock to her when something prompted her to inquire where he slept at night She imagined vaguely that he slept on the beach or in some cave.

For the last week he had been sleeping in Queenie's hut, it appeared. Prudence knew Queenie by sight. She was a coarse native woman, no longer young. That it

81

was for the convenience of the hut rather than for the charms of Queenie did not lessen the horror of it to Prudence. She regarded this as the beachcomber's final degradation.

'How could you!' she exclaimed.

'Well, beggars can't be choosers. I'm not grumbling. She's a good-hearted old bitch, really; she's been kind to me and looked after me. I would have been damned-awful hungry sometimes, if it had not been for her: she never grudges me a meal.'

'But how could you?' she repeated, screwing up her face in disgust.

'You are talking nonsense, my dear, if I may say so. No one would rather starve who has any experience of it.'

'Very likely not. Perhaps we English are more sensitive.'

'To me it is nothing. A man, whatever the colour of his skin, is my brother the same as a Russian.'

'Don't try to convince me that you look on Queenie as a sister!'

'It's funny how vulgar the most refined become when they are angry.'

'I'm not angry. I'm revolted!' she said witheringly. 'You are evidently incapable of grasping that, because the gulf between us is so wide. *I* believe that integrity should come before everything.'

'Integrity?' He wrinkled his nose. 'Is it nobler to sleep in the open night air and get malaria or some other fever and die of it? You must admit, my sensible Proodance, that it is not very practical.'

'You have no moral fibre,' she sighed. 'I was almost beginning to have confidence in you, so it is just as well that I found you out before I began to make a proper fool of myself,' she added bitterly. 'If I found you somewhere else to sleep, would you go? Or do you prefer Queenie's companionship to mine?'

He gazed at her intently, feeling the first elated stirrings of hope.

'There is absolutely no reason for you to be jealous, darling,' he assured her. 'I will leave her tomorrow — today, if you like. I would much, much rather sleep alone — if I cannot sleep with you, of course,' he added civilly . . .

At the foot of the hill on the Carib Bay

side was a tiny creek, on the edge of which Jacques had erected a little bathing hut quite near their old villa. Since Julia's illness it had scarcely been used. Probably it was no longer watertight, but the rains were still a long way off. It was a neat, wooden structure, the outside laboriously painted to resemble brick, with imitation windows and a trellis-work of painted roses blooming statically about the door. Inside, it was fitted up chintzily enough to be a home from home for Boris. She thought she could manage to get a key for him, and if he was reasonably cautious he was not likely to be discovered. What did he think of the idea?

He stared at her blankly, incredulously, for a minute, and then laughed.

'I don't see why not.'

'Then, you shall have the key as soon as possible,' she promised.

Prudence was satisfied that she had saved him from a dishonour worse than death; and though she did not realise it, she liked to weave chains of obligation about him. For his part, Boris was glad of the solitude. To have a house eight feet by four feet all to himself was a kind of luxury after all, even though he dared not show a light or be less quiet than the proverbial mouse.

Now that they were not so very far apart, she would sometimes steal down when she guessed him to be there and bring him odds and ends of food, or a thermos full of coffee, and they would have a midnight picnic, silently, by the light of the stars. But that was not very often. For if her malevolent old witch of an employer ever discovered her nocturnal absences there would be every kind of a rumpus, she explained.

Boris was her safety-valve for that, too. She was able to let off steam about Hattie and how afraid she sometimes felt.

So their nomad idyll continued.

5

There's a Hoodoo on Voodoo

The Foleys' bungalow was on Palm Point, the other side of Carib Bay. It was gracefully decorated in a judicious blending of native materials and European style.

It was some days after their first meeting that they invited Quentin there to lunch on a day when Foley knew that he would not be on the plantation.

The conversation drifted naturally enough to the Jacqueses.

It was an odd affair, no denying it, and yet it was not possible to put one's finger on any precise . . .

It was funny how unalike the sisters had been in every imaginable way. Julia, much younger than Hattie, had been the handsome one. That, and the fact that she was married, was why their father's money had been left to Hattie. Fair enough! Hattie was well-off, and she was likely the richest planter on the Island. So there was no reason why Julia should have left her anything but the few trinkets she sentimentally did. No, Julia's money came from an aunt and was left to her unconditionally. She ought, perhaps, to have left her money to her husband whom she loved, but very likely she thought he was sufficiently covered by his job and the pension he would receive on retiring.

'I wonder what young Raoul thinks about it all?' said Foley, as they sat at lunch.

'Rather poor view of it, I believe,' said Mr. Seal cautiously. 'They say he feels that there has been some funny business on the part of Father Xavier.'

'There may be something in what he says. They're rum beggars, these priests. Wasn't there some kind of hocus-pocus with the cats? The priest put one in her room or something, or so I heard.'

'The nurse said she saw him bring it *out* of Madame's room. But your idea is that he would do it for the money that he may have known was willed to him?'

suggested Mr. Seal.

'Darling, do be careful,' said Evelyn hastily. 'I'm sure that's libellous,'

'It's only between ourselves. Well, if the priest did it and he can get away with it, good luck to him! It'll do that young whippersnapper all the good in the world to have to earn his own bread. Of course, if he'd been brought up in a decent English public school, he'd have turned out very different. But, as it is, he's actually more French than English — '

'Poor Johnny,' his wife laughed, 'he has an obsession about English superiority.'

'It's that young blackguard I've got an obsession about,' growled Foley. 'I only wish you had seen him the other night, Seal, when we went there to dinner. At least, we went to Miss Brown's and he was there, and his father and that secretary girl. What a spectacle! My God! The way he was behaving with his aunt was beyond description, like one of these damned gigolos. It was enough to turn one's stomach!'

'It wasn't that, so much as the animals.' Evelyn shuddered. 'She really is a disgusting old woman. I don't know how Johnny can put up with her.'

'I'm used to her. I hardly notice the animals any more. But it is a bit sickening.'

'She lets them feed at the table, you know, and eat out of her plate. Actually, I saw her break off a lump of candied ham in a cat's mouth and stuff it into her own. I couldn't eat a thing after that.'

'Altogether, not the most enjoyable evening, eh?'

'Even old Jacques got a bit fed up in the end, I think. I'm sure he made Raoul escort Eve home simply because he couldn't endure to see him playing up to his aunt that way. I had to stay and talk business with her — she's my boss, and Eve wanted to get home, and she made out that she had a bad head. So young jackanapes Jacques was detailed to take her back. And *then* what do you think happened? Go on, tell him, Eve!'

'Don't be such a fool, John. There was nothing in it at all. Have some of these persimmons, Mr. Seal, they're home-grown.'

'I don't wonder it makes you blush, old girl — a woman old enough to be his mother.'

'I'm not blushing, but if I were it would be because of your bad taste. Please consider our guest.'

'It'll give him a laugh! Listen, Seal. Poor hard-working hubby toddles home to wifie about midnight and finds her locked in our young friend's arms. What do you think of *that*? What a young bounder, eh? I told him off P.D.Q., I assure you.'

'Johnny makes such a fuss about nothing. He's absurdly jealous. The silly kid just lost his head for a moment. I daresay his aunt's flattery and too much to drink was at the back of it.'

'Isn't she a modest little thing! Anyway, I hoofed him out all right. I don't care to have anyone mucking about with my wife. How he howled when he felt my boot on his backside! He needs a few more like that.'

'That's enough, Johnny. What an old bore you are!' said his wife.

Quentin mused privately on the pleasures of married life. To change the subject, he admired the emerald and diamond clips on the neck of her silk frock.

'I noticed them at the funeral,' he said. 'They really are very fine.'

'They are pretty,' she agreed carelessly. 'How are you liking the Royal Splendide?'

'I don't believe I've seen them before,' said Johnny. 'Where did you get 'em? Don't tell me I gave 'em to you myself for an anniversary or something.'

'That would be too much of a good thing,' she said bitingly. 'You gave me a pair of silk stockings last year. If you must know, I bought them myself.'

'Since when have you been a woman of wealth?'

'I really don't know what's got into you today, John. Am I to account for every penny I manage to save out of the housekeeping? God knows I don't have much pleasure, and I haven't noticed you overwhelming me with presents. I've bought one for myself, and I'm dashed if I can see why there should have to be a post-mortem in front of our guest, and over something that only cost a couple of hundred francs. It's ridiculous!'

'Two hundred francs? Twenty thousand, more like!'

'Oh, don't be a fool. Where would I get twenty thousand francs from?'

'That's what I'd like to know. I don't pretend to know anything about jewellery, but they look the real McCoy to me. What do you say, Seal?'

'I should say — ' began Quentin; he was cut short by a foot pressing lightly on his, and raised his eyes to see the flash of frantic appeal in hers. ' — they were a very fine imitation,' he concluded.

'That's why I bought them. They were too good an opportunity to miss. I got them from Valere's, John; why don't you go in and ask them what I paid?'

'Now the little woman's cross. Are you married, Seal?'

'No,' said Quentin, in unconsciously heartfelt tones.

'Lucky devil! Well, if you'll excuse me!' He rose to his feet. 'Got to get back to the grindstone, I guess.' He ruffled his wife's hair the wrong way as he passed. 'Still, I wouldn't be without the wife, Gorblesser!

We understand one another, don't we, Eve?' He kissed the back of her neck.

'Run along, silly!' she said, patting his cheek. 'Shall we have coffee on the veranda?' She rose, Quentin following her. When they were settled on the wooden porch and had waved goodbye to Foley, she turned to him gratefully.

'Thank you for your tact,' she said. 'Johnny's insanely jealous. I don't take any notice of it now, it doesn't mean anything. Raoul is just a kid who lost his mother a few days before; he wanted comforting, that's all. And then Johnny had to come in and make an exhibition of himself. Oh, well, what does it matter! I'm getting as tiresome as he is. Forgive me!'

'My dear Mrs. Foley!' protested Mr. Seal. And begged that he might look at the troublesome clips. They were real, all right; the setting was unmistakable. 'If they didn't cost you more than twenty thousand, I should judge you had a bargain.'

'I adore emeralds,' she smiled, 'I've been saving for years, and then I had a little windfall besides. I didn't tell Johnny. He'd only have found some other use for it. Well, so I saw these in Valere's, and I simply couldn't resist them. But, after all, jewels always fetch their value, and it's portable property; if I ever wanted to — oh, I don't know — run away, perhaps . . . Not that I would. Poor Johnny would die without me.'

'Wasn't it a little unwise to tell him where you got them?'

'I've told them what to say if he should come in. These places never mind making a faked receipt; they seem to take it quite as a matter of course. I suppose more of this kind of deception goes on than one would imagine. Still, it makes life so much more peaceful that it's worth the little extra trouble.'

It didn't seem very simple to Quentin. There was not much of her story that he believed — and he was pretty sure they had cost more than twenty thousand. It was amusing to watch her lie and parry, and enlightening to hear her husband nag, growling and barking, but never biting. But if he was like a dog, she was

94

like a cat. A cat-and-dog life, mused Quentin. Drowsily, fragments of a nursery jingle came back to him. ' . . . The dog that worried the cat . . . ' What was it? 'The cat — that killed the rat . . . something or other . . . that lay in the house that Jack built.' That was funny, wasn't it? What about the rest of it? 'The maiden all forlorn . . . ' That was Miss Whitaker, of course; and so the cow with the crumpled horn was obviously Miss Brown . . . He chuckled sleepily as he pieced it together.

When he left Evelyn, Mr. Seal went over to the church, ostensibly sightseeing. The church was plaster in the baroque style with a top-heavy campanile in pink stucco. Inside, he was interested to note that the pew ends were decorated with native carvings. Father Xavier saw him and greeted him cheerily.

'Come back with me and I will give you a cup of English tea,' he offered, and Quentin agreed.

The priest's house was not five minutes' walk from the church — a little lath-and-plaster bungalow, practically bare beyond the necessary chairs and tables and rickety camp-beds.

Father Xavier walked over to his writing-table and turned over the little pile of envelopes.

'Will you excuse me,' he begged, slitting an envelope as he spoke with a neat little stiletto. 'It's the European mail. It means so much to an exile, you know . . . '

Tactfully, Quentin strolled out to admire his tiny garden. There were trim rows of vegetables, struggling gallantly against the sun. And flowers in formal borders, marigolds and zinnias, whose tints repeated the glories of the sunset sky. Presently the priest joined him. The cool evening breeze arose as the sun disappeared, and they drank it in grate-fully, watching the stars prick through the blue velvet.

There was an eerie shriek from the house — a figure came flying towards them and flung itself prone at the priest's feet, yelling and chattering.

'What on earth . . . ?' The priest stooped down and shook the young house-boy's shoulder. His eyeballs gleamed white with terror in his black face.

'Duppy — duppy — ' he sobbed. 'In your room — ah, see it, *Mon Père* — !'

The priest yanked him to his feet.

'Pull yourself together. There are no such things as duppies, Georges.'

'*Ouais, Mon Père.*' He crossed himself hastily. 'But that's what I see just now!'

'Well, we'll go and have a look for ourselves — Mr. Seal, please hold his other arm; he's like an eel — you're coming with us to show us just what it was you saw, and where.'

Of course, when they arrived, there was nothing to be seen — neither ghost nor sheeted figure. Nothing! Father Xavier shrugged.

'Whose duppy was it?'

'La Morte's,' Georges said sullenly, and crossed himself again.

'All right,' said Father Xavier, releasing him. 'Get out, now. And if I hear that you've breathed one word of this to anyone else, there's going to be such trouble that a mere duppy will seem like indigestion to you, see? Get along,

97

Georges, and don't be a fool again.'

The priest exchanged a meaningful glance with Quentin and shrugged as the boy departed.

'I wish there was some way of keeping that idiot's mouth shut, but there isn't, of course; the story will be blabbed all over the Island.'

'Isn't 'duppy' a West Indian word for 'ghost'?'

'It means a departed spirit who for some reason — out of revenge or something — returns to haunt a place or a person. So my duppy is La Morte, as they used to call the poor soul. I suppose she wants her money back. I wonder why?'

'You don't believe in it, surely?'

'I don't think I do. I can't help feeling that if she means to haunt me, she might at least have had the courtesy to wait till I arrived on the scene. It seems a little impromptu.'

'You think someone wanted to scare you? I wonder how they fixed it,' mused Seal.

'Perhaps they simply bribed Georges to

make it up. Shall we have a drink? I feel I could do with one — it's upset me a little, but not quite in the way they intended, perhaps.'

'I don't think Georges was making it all up. He seemed genuinely scared to me.'

Father Xavier tipped up the round-bellied rum bottle till the last dark drops trickled into the glasses.

'Well, I don't know how they stage-managed it, then. I wonder whether it would have taken me in.'

'It was rather silly of whoever it was to imagine that you would be scared of a ghost, wasn't it? What did they hope to gain by it?'

'Your health!' He tipped back his head. 'My dear Mr. Seal, you know my enemies over this business as well as I do myself. We know who is angry about the money, who feels I have no right to it and probably acquired it under false pretences. Well, they want to frighten me into surrendering it, I imagine, spreading rumours about me so that people get it into their heads that Madame Jacques never wanted me to have the money. To make it so dreadfully uncomfortable for me that I actually would be morally forced to give it up.'

'What a twisted mentality!'

'But it's so stupid,' said the priest. 'Money means less than nothing to me. But they don't seem able to grasp that the money has been left to me *in trust* for the greater glory of God. Of course I won't give it up. Why should I?'

'Of course,' Quentin agreed vaguely. 'But how do you intend to counteract this activity against you?'

'Oh dear, I don't know. I suppose the Lord is tempting me.'

'You're quite sure it couldn't possibly have been a duppy?'

Father Xavier smiled faintly, and made no reply beyond raising his eyebrows in quizzical semicircles.

★   ★   ★

As it happened, Father Xavier had not been so very far out in his calculations. This was one of the links in the chain of circumstances binding Raoul and his aunt in sudden intimacy. They both benefited from the relationship. Hattie was far wealthier than his parents, and she promised, with plenty of cajolery, to be as soft and doting as his mother. She knew a thing or two besides, did the old girl, and he had high hopes that she would somehow wangle the money away from the priest. And Hattie *was* flattered by him, there was no denying it: he was so pretty, and young, and quite a lad already, but wide open to further corruption. It amused her immensely to feel she had a young thing's character to mould. She was going to have a considerable influence over him: It was something to look forward to. Also, it tickled her to death to play him off against other people; she loved to see Jacques' temper rise as she flirted with ludicrous ostentation with his son, or Evelyn Foley's; even Prudence had been seen to flush with disgust. It was fun, and there were so few things that amused her nowadays.

'You leave it to Old Aunt Hattie,' she would say, stroking his sleek golden hair. 'She'll see that dirty old priest doesn't get away with your money.'

'What'll you do, Auntie?' he would beg prettily, as a child begs for a favourite story.

'We'll harry him and persecute him till he doesn't know which way to turn and feels that every man's hand is against him. It'll be all the easier if he's got a bad conscience, as I dare say he has. That's only the beginning — that's child's play. If that doesn't have any effect, there are other, more telling means. Much more amusing for us,' she promised, 'and much nastier for him.'

But what these were, she would not vouchsafe even to him. The next day, Mr. Seal steeled himself to make the dreadful climb to the house; his excuse was that he wanted to see Hattie and ask her if she knew anything about voodoo. He was interested in the obscurer manifestations of religion. And it seemed to him just possible that she would be able to inform him about its existence on the Island.

He walked in unannounced as usual and passed through one empty room after another, as littered and untidy as before the grand funeral. Cats sprawled indolently in all directions. In one room he came upon Prudence standing tiptoe on a chair, peering curiously into an earthenware pot almost hidden on the top of an antique Flemish cupboard. She swung round with a startled white face and a cry of terror. She swayed vertiginously, and he ran forward to catch her as she fell.

Now, why, he mused, as he laid her on the bed and looked around for water, *why scream and faint because someone makes you jump?*

He splashed a few drops of water from the ewer in the basin onto her white face. Perhaps the door had been left open in order to hear approaching footsteps, and then in her absorption they had come unheard. It would be interesting to know what lay in the pot.

Hastily, he climbed on the chair. It was an ordinary earthenware flowerpot filled with earth. There was no reason for a young woman to faint because she was caught looking to see whether the bulb she had planted was coming up. He poked an exploratory forefinger in the earth, and withdrew it almost at once with a sharp exclamation. Cautiously brushing away the earth, he saw something gleaming, and caught sight of a repulsive purplish shiny object stuck with needles. Before he could investigate further, he heard a faint fluttery moan, and leapt off his perch. He knelt beside Prudence, patting her hand, and surreptitiously sucking his injured forefinger. Why keep a pincushion in a flowerpot?

'It's all right, Miss Whitaker. Don't move. I'll go and find Miss Brown.' Her fingers scrabbled at his sleeve.

'No, no, please don't,' she said fearfully. 'It was nothing . . . the sudden heat . . . I'd really much rather you didn't bother Miss Brown. It would only make her angry.'

'What are you afraid of, Miss Whitaker?'

'Nothing at all, Mr. Seal. Please let me get up now — I'm quite all right — and I'll go and tell Miss Brown you're here.'

'You don't have to be afraid of *me*, you know.'

'Honestly, it's all right.' She stood up.

'Come into the parlour-room, while I find her. And I really must apologise for fainting all over you. This climate doesn't really agree with me.'

There was nothing to do but follow her.

In the large circular room inside the tower, she pushed a cat out of a cane chair and fluffed up the cushions for him.

'I'd rather you didn't mention it to Miss Brown. She'd fuss and think I was ill or something . . . and really, everything's difficult enough already,' she sighed, as she departed.

'Voodoo!' screeched Miss Brown. 'How perfectly killing!' Her breasts shook with laughter. 'I should have thought you were old enough to know better, Mr. Seal.' She smoothed her dress over her fat thighs and sniggered. 'Do you believe in fairies, Mr. Seal?'

Quentin smiled at her good-humouredly,

'Speaking personally, I like to keep an open mind on such matters. As for voodooism, that's another thing altogether. It isn't a question of belief, my dear Miss Brown, but of simple curiosity. My craft as a writer, you know . . .

'The Island must be full of old superstitions and so forth, and it occurred to me that you might be able to help me find out a bit about it, or advise me where I can get some information on the subject.'

'Well, I can't,' she said amiably. 'And you won't find yourself best liked if you go around asking awkward questions. I think you'll find that most of them are as ignorant and disinterested as I am.'

'Do you mean to tell me,' he said incredulously, 'that no book has been written on the subject? Has no one been here? Scientific investigators? Anthropologists?'

'We are a very simple unspoilt people. We are all Christians now, and believe in progress,' said Hattie, with an unbelievably smug expression. 'If there ever was any voodooism or black magic or other kind of witchcraft on the Island, it was a very long time ago and we prefer not to think about it. With our superior education, we understand now that it was merely superstitious nonsense — quite powerless, of course, but evil nevertheless.'

He strolled over to the window.

'It's all so confusing . . . *You* say it's nonsense and no longer exists, anyway; and yet only yesterday some native boy saw a duppy in the priest's house.'

'Ho, ho, ho! So that's what put the bee in your bonnet, eh? And what did dear Father Xavier have to say?'

'He didn't believe it.'

'But you, on the contrary, like to think that *there are more things in heaven and earth* — and hell, too, for that matter . . .'

'You don't ask whose duppy it was,' he commented. 'It was your sister's.'

She nodded thoughtfully.

'I suppose I might have guessed that.'

Silence. The conversation seemed to have petered out. He pressed the little red wound on his forefinger against his mouth, pensively. He was longing to have another look inside that pot, but he couldn't think of an excuse to get rid of her. Well, he supposed he could always bully it out of the timid secretary. He sighed, and took his leave.

'Come again soon,' said Hattie cheerfully. 'You make me laugh. Come to dinner tomorrow night. And I'll make my brother-in-law come, too; it'll do him good to laugh a little. He's too serious. It's his condition, I suppose. He's diabetic, and it makes him languid and gloomy. We'll see if we can't cheer him up, eh?'

That, was that.

Mr. Seal sat on the raised sidewalk outside the Royal Splendide drinking his *aperitif* with a shabby fellow, an obvious 'character' that he had picked up — or, rather, who had picked up him. He was a beachcomber, with a quaint accent and rather amusing ways. Borodin, he said his name was. It was odd that they had not met one another before.

Once he was loosened up with liquor, Quentin began to hint about his interest in voodoo. Had Borodin ever been to a seance, or whatever they called it? Borodin assured him garrulously that he knew all there was to know about such things, that he was practically the Big Chief himself.

Then did he know of any such doings on the Island?

'The Island is full of it,' he declared. 'Obeah in every hut. Truly, I tell you.'

But as soon as Quentin pressed him for further details, he said that he had been boasting really, and that nowadays he was sure it did not amount to more than sickening off a neighbour's hens or causing a crop to fail. Nothing really dangerous or harmful.

Quentin pinned him down to a promise that he would find out when the very next ceremonial affair was, and that he would take Quentin to it.

'When I come back,' he said. 'I think I am going away for a few days, but when I come back. Honestly.'

The conversation then lapsed into a guarded haggling over the price. They closed the deal finally for seventy-five francs, and parted on the best of terms.

6

Dinner with Miss Brown

Mr. Seal toiled up to the castle, regretting that he had accepted the invitation to dinner. The last rays of the sun illumined the ancient walls and turned the flagged courtyard to a vibrant rose. Quentin paused to admire the scene. Something caught his eye.

Almost in the middle of the courtyard lay the flowerpot, smashed to pieces and half-covered with the released soil it had contained. He bent and stirred it gently with his finger, but there was only the brown earth and red earthenware.

As usual, the front door was open, guarded only by a striped canvas curtain. He pushed this aside and went into the house. There were voices raised as if in anger, and he went down the dim corridor towards them.

'You brute, you vile brute! Now I

110

understand what you're really like,' he heard Hattie cry passionately. And then she added in a crooning wail: 'Oh, my darling, Mummy's poor little darling! There, there!'

'I didn't do it, Auntie, I didn't!' Raoul replied feverishly. 'Why don't you believe me?'

Quentin hesitated; he could hardly barge in on a family quarrel. He moved a step nearer into a shadowy alcove and waited.

'Because I saw you with my own eyes,' Hattie resumed. 'You cruel little swine! But I'll get my own back on you for this! My God, I will! I'd like to carve you into little pieces by hand.' And then, with a change of tone: 'My little sweet, my rose of Sharon, what have they done to you!'

'But, Auntie, you're wrong, honestly. I ran out just before you did to try and prevent it. Why should I want to do such a thing? Be reasonable, for God's sake, darling! I don't know what has happened. We have always got on so well, and now suddenly it is all tears and temper.'

His voice grew more and more tender.

'Let us kiss and make up,' he murmured, and added something in tones inaudible to the eavesdropper a few yards away.

'Be quiet, you devil!' she shrieked. 'I'll have no more to do with you. I'm through. I shall never, never forgive you. Heaven knows I have no conscience worth speaking of, but there is only one word for what you've done, and that's — *murder*! I draw the line at that.' He tried to interrupt her, but she shouted him down irresistibly. 'You'll be punished, never fear. The devil looks after his own . . . A life for a life.'

'Well, for God's sake don't make such a row about it. Do you want the whole of Wigtown to hear you? And I should have thought you were the last person — the very last person — to talk about *murder*,' he snarled, his tender veneer stripped away. 'If some people knew what I know — my God!'

'It's too late to try and blackmail me now, damn you — too late, too late . . . ' The keening recommenced: 'Oh, oh, oh! He's gone — he's gone!'

'May I inquire what is going on here?'

asked a third voice dispassionately, which after a second Quentin recognised to be Jacques'.

There was a momentary silence, which Quentin conjectured to be filled with fear and surprise. At last, Hattie remarked in her usual high, shrill voice:

'Why, Antoine, where ever did you spring from? You startled me!'

'Where else but upstairs, Hattie, my dear.'

'But I didn't know you were in. I thought you . . . Why didn't you come down before?' she expostulated.

'Had you forgotten that the court doesn't sit this afternoon?'

'Then you have been in all the time?' Was there a note of panic in her voice?

'Actually, no. I went to confession this afternoon . . . and afterwards I was kept longer than I expected. Which reminds me, Raoul: I wish to speak to you — later.'

'Yes, Papa.'

'But what has happened, pray?'

'Nothing, Antoine. I shall ring for Josef to remove him.'

The sound of an electric bell made Quentin tense. He glanced round hurriedly. The servant must not see him. He pushed wider a wedged-open door and slipped in quickly, as soft steps padded nearer along the passage. In a minute, the servant returned down the dim corridor, bearing something in his arms — to Quentin's annoyance, it was impossible to see what.

Jacques was saying: 'I prefer to tell you later and listen to your explanations when I have more leisure. Very likely it will not be tonight at all. Were you intending to go out tonight, Raoul?'

'Er — no, Papa. I was going to spend the evening quietly in my room studying for my exams — I have less than a month now.'

'Oh, I'm glad that *has* occurred to you! I was beginning to wonder whether there was anything in the world you took seriously. Very well, then, go upstairs, and please remain there till I return. You understand?'

'Yes, Papa.' Pause.

'Don't you say good night to your

aunt?' said Jacques irritably.

'Good night, Aunt,' came the meek voice.

Quentin waited for him to pass — which he did, with a fiendishly contorted face — and then stepped authoritatively into the passage.

Hattie greeted him cordially, if rather absently, and Jacques began gravely mixing drinks — according to taste. There was a rather boring interchange of chit-chat.

Jacques handed Hattie a mint-julep.

'What exactly was the trouble just now, my dear? Has that boy been annoying you?'

'He has, Antoine. He really goes too far. I don't want to think about it, it upsets me too much. I can deal with it myself. I shan't let it pass. Trust me.'

'He's getting beyond me,' sighed Jacques. 'When I think of the damage he does, I almost feel afraid. How can I prevent it, Hattie? Is it my fault? I used to imagine that he was such a good boy — a bit wild, perhaps, with the wildness of youth; but good, *au fond*. But now, since his mother's death ... Of course, she used to spoil him, but it only meant that I was a bit stricter with him in compensation. Yet now I begin to wonder how he can come to be my son ... I'm so sorry, Mr. Seal, this is so boring for you.'

'Not at all. He is at the awkward adolescent stage, complicated by his recent bereavement. I dare say he hardly knows what he's doing half the time himself.'

'It's kind of you to make excuses for him,' said Jacques. 'But he has no excuse for attacking the good little Father Xavier. He asked to speak with me privately after confession today. So I went to his house. I thought he was looking very poorly. Had you heard about it, Hattie? Apparently he had suffered a heart attack as well, which he could not but put down to Raoul's behaviour, too. That a son of mine should ... I felt humiliated. Of course, I apologised most profusely, and promised I would talk to him severely, but how can one punish a thing like that? I could cheerfully kill him for putting me in such a position and creating such a scandal. I suppose by now it's all over Wigtown — all over Apostle, probably.'

'Poor Antoine, you do look quite fagged out, and no wonder. What a little wretch he has become! Though perhaps I was a little to blame about the priest. I did encourage him rather, I'm afraid. But then I never meant him to take things into his own hands like that. Young fiend . . . '

'That isn't all. Who do you think was at Father Xavier's house, waiting to see him? Your bailiff, Foley. At first he didn't seem best pleased to see *me*. But then he said he wanted to talk to me and would wait for me to finish with the priest and would then walk back with me . . . Will you have another drink, Mr. Seal? And you, my dear . . . ? Well, this wretched Englishman began a rigmarole about Raoul and his wife. He had come home one evening and found them together. He kicked Raoul out, of course, and told him that if ever he caught him hanging round his wife again he would half-kill him. He said he thought at the time that he had scared him out of his life, but now he was

117

beginning to wonder if they weren't contriving to meet secretly. And the thought was driving him mad, tied as he was to his work. He begged me to speak to Raoul seriously.

'Twice in one day! You can imagine how I felt. Of course, it was wrong of Raoul; but, as I pointed out to Foley, with a woman twice his age it was unlikely that he was the sole culprit or that the initial moves had come from him. That didn't please Foley — he evidently likes to think his wife is purer than the lily of the valley, or perhaps it was too close to the truth to be agreeable. He asked me again to warn my son. I agreed, but begged him also to warn his wife. We parted on bad terms. I don't *like* that man, Hattie, and I never shall. Fancy not being able to control his wife and admitting it openly. Fancy being cuckolded by a boy of eighteen! Not that I exonerate Raoul from blame on that account. It's very, very wrong of him. That's three people he's upset today, not counting me.'

'Well, don't upset yourself any further tonight. Let us just enjoy our supper,'

Hattie suggested soothingly.

'Moreover,' said Quentin helpfully, 'I was given to understand that it was nothing worth mentioning, the business between your son and Mrs. Foley. It was one night when he saw her home from here, I understood, and then rather lost his head and kissed her at the very moment Mr. Foley walked in.'

'You really think it was no more than that? Well, I shall put it out of my mind now, and trust that tomorrow will bring wisdom and inspiration. I'm not particularly anxious for him to grow up a criminal — not very becoming in a judge's son, is it? You've been very kind and patient, and I really do feel happier now that I've shared my woes with you all.' He smiled. 'I suppose I'm as ludicrous as that absurd Foley, really.'

Dinner was in the tower-room, always the coolest room in the house because it was in real old walls, the window embrasures four feet deep. Candles flamed stiffly motionless in antique sconces on the table. Iced pawpaw stood in high-stemmed glasses invitingly.

'And you write, I understand, Mr. Seal?' said Jacques politely.

'I don't have any literary pretensions. I'm a mere hack, hard-working and crafty, earning my living by the sweat of my brow. The fantasies I scribble are devoid of style, philosophy or beauty. But, on the other hand, they are highly moral, for evil never pays and is always uncovered on the last page; the criminal is punished and truth is brilliantly triumphant. I recommend myself to mercy, your honour.'

Quentin hung his head and acknowledged ten previous offences.

'Oh, he's altogether too humble, my dear. His detective stories are best-sellers, translated into every imaginable language,' laughed Hattie. 'In fact, one might almost say you're colleagues, in a manner of speaking.'

'So we might. The case is dismissed with scarcely a stain on the prisoner's noble character. I wish I could say I had read some of your books, but I'm afraid — '

'Don't apologise. I've never heard you try a case yet, so we're quits.'

'Have you always written?'

'No, I used to be in an insurance-broker's office, my head buried in a desk for fifty weeks a year. Never went anywhere, never saw anything. Then one day I woke up. Like a fairy princess! What was I waiting for? I was thirty-five. If I had only one life to live, I was damn well not going to waste another minute of it. I walked out there and then and never went back.' He laughed.

'But what did you *do*?' asked Hattie.

'Starved a little at first. My savings totalled just twenty-three pounds. My difficulty at first was that I wasn't quite sure what I wanted to do. I'm lazy by temperament, and easily bored. So I did various odd jobs, but never sticking at anything for long. I worked my way round the world on cargo. Yet, glamorous though it was, I wasn't really satisfied; there was so much hard work and very little freedom. I didn't seem any better off than I was before. Then, some five or six years ago, I was in Malaya and I heard a story that intrigued me. It was unfinished, and I used to tease myself by imagining possible solutions. I thought, if it interested me, it ought to interest someone else. I wrote it down . . . and thus began my despicable career of crime,' he concluded lightly.

Josef served chicken stuffed with tender little yellow plums. Mr. Seal congratulated Hattie on her cook. A comfortable, satisfying silence reigned for a few minutes.

It was broken by a scream that made them all jump nervously. Orlando, the gibbon, was bouncing angrily up and down in the window, pushing against the wire netting in a frantic attempt to get in.

'All right, Hattie, I'll let him in,' said Jacques. 'Sit still.' He undid the catch and swung the netting open. The gibbon rushed in, bickering with himself.

'Mother's boy!' exclaimed Hattie passionately and folded him to her capacious bosom. 'Thank you, Antoine . . . What is it?' she added, as he started back with an exclamation. But before he had time to answer, she gave a cry of dismay and rose to her feet. 'A moth!'

'Yes, it flew into my face and startled

me,' said Jacques.

'It's a death's head, I do declare,' remarked Quentin.

'Oh, get it out! I can't *bear* them,' Hattie cried, watching with horrified eyes as the huge furry creature fluttered and swooped about the candle flames. 'Whatever did you let it in for, Antoine? You know I'm terrified of them.'

'My dear, I didn't let it in on purpose. And it was at your request that I opened the netting,' Jacques reminded her stiffly.

'Well, shut it now, goddamnit, before any more fly in!'

She tucked the gibbon securely under one arm and flicked at the moth again with her napkin. 'I'm not superstitious . . . but a death's head, *really*,' she muttered, shuddering.

Quentin tactfully suggested that she should retire from the fray and leave it to him. Obediently, she retreated to the door and beyond, and waited . . .

In a minute, Quentin called out that it was all over. She came back, rather shame-faced. 'I know it's ridiculous, but I've been the same all my life. Antoine dear, forgive me for behaving like an ill-tempered sow.'

'Don't mention it.'

Hattie shot a contrite glance at him as she resumed her seat.

Dinner was recommenced, but the easy atmosphere was gone. Hattie was jumpy and Jacques absent-minded. At last, Hattie rose to leave the gentlemen to their port. With the gibbon on her arm, she sauntered from the room.

'I'll go and see how Prude is getting on, and whether she's had any dinner — if not, whether she wants any,' she remarked.

Jacques waited till she was out of sight and hearing, and then raised a forefinger importantly:

'Wait! I am going to fetch you something that will melt your heart with its magnificence. My sister-in-law is a marvellous woman in many ways, but she does not understand *port*. I would not offend her by telling her that the stuff she offers us is undrinkable — I will simply get something of my own that defies description. Will you excuse me for just five minutes?'

Alone, Quentin at once became immersed in his thoughts. He glanced at his watch. It was a quarter to ten.

At length Jacques came in, napkin on arm, bearing carefully a dusty bottle in a wicker cradle. He set it down and slowly withdrew the cork. Tiny beads stood out on his forehead and his lips were drawn in with the strain. He ran the napkin gently round the neck of the bottle. Then he tilted the basket slightly and the wine poured slow, thick, and dark into the glass. He tossed the stained napkin away and handed the glass to the other.

Quentin held it to the flame for its colour, and to his nose for the bouquet. He waited for Jacques' glass to fill up. Jacques smiled.

'A wine like this needs no toast to commend it.'

There was a tapping at the wire screen leading to the terrace on the south side. Hattie stood silhouetted massively against the night sky. Mr. Seal hastened to let her in. She was breathing rather quickly, he thought, and her nostrils were white. She advanced into the room without speaking and sank into a chair.

'That girl!' she said at last.

'What is it, dear?' Jacques' voice sounded a little nervous. He began to drink quickly, as though he was afraid she would notice the port and be angry.

'Listen. She asked to be excused from dinner tonight. Said she had a headache — I don't know, it's always something — anyway, she didn't want any supper, only wanted to be allowed to go to bed,' Hattie said rapidly. 'Of course, I let her. She's not such a social asset anyway. So, in the goodness of my heart, I go along to see if she needs anything — ' She paused furiously.

'Well?'

'The door was locked, as usual. I don't know what she's afraid of, or who she thinks would want to come in. However, I called: no answer. I knocked: still no answer. Why?'

'Asleep,' Mr. Seal volunteered brilliantly.

'Dead,' Jacques suggested mildly, by a natural sequence of ideas.

'It was simpler than that!' Hattie

snapped. 'She just wasn't there.'

'Oh!' No one was very interested.

'Don't you see, she could have just asked me? But she had to make a great mystery out of it for some reason, and lie, and lock her door in a vain attempt to keep the truth from me. Heavens, how I loathe subterfuge!'

'How did you find out, by the way?'

'I knew damn well she wasn't asleep. So I went round the outside and tried the shutters, which were closed — to suggest she was lying in the dark — and they came open quite easily. All she had to do was lock the door and slip out through the shutters, closing them carefully behind her, at a time when she knew we would be at dinner.'

'Where's she gone, then?'

'My dear Antoine, how do you expect me to know?'

'Then why so angry about it, dear?'

'It's the deceit. Why climb out of the window unless one has something to conceal?'

Jacques frowned. 'I must say it does seem strange,' he said slowly. 'For argument's sake, if it was not a lover who whisked her away so secretively, what else could it be, do you imagine?'

No one knew the answer to that.

'What are you going to do about it, anyway? Haul her over the coals tomorrow?'

Hattie gave a feline smile and shook her head.

'I shall watch,' she said, with the slow patience of a cat waiting over a mousehole. 'When I know why she does it, I shall know how to deal with it.'

Quentin's sympathy was with Miss Whitaker.

They adjourned to the dusty parlour, and the conversation drifted into other channels.

John Foley came into the room, hesitated at the sight of the company, and would have backed out but that Miss Brown insisted he stay.

'I'm awfully sorry, I had no idea you were entertaining tonight. But you particularly asked me to call.'

'Did I?' said Hattie vaguely. 'You'll have something to take now you're here?'

'No, thanks. You wanted to see the export accounts, porterage and cargo-charges and so on. Don't you remember?'

'I believe I do. It's no matter. Anyway, now you've brought them, I can have a look at them if you like. But first of all you must have something to take; you're looking all-in.'

'I'm filthy. I must apologise. But by the time I finished, it was so late I didn't like to stop to change. I'm quite sure I look a wreck.'

He was right, he did. His hair was dishevelled, and his open-necked shirt and khaki shorts were stained, and crumpled with the day's work. His hands were grubby and his face white and sweaty. He really did look pretty done up.

Quentin tactfully rose to go. It seemed kindest to let the poor chap get his work done and go home to bed. He bade them all a civil goodnight and left.

7

And Sudden Death

Halfway down the Jacob's ladder, Quentin paused to listen to light footsteps running towards him. A slim shadow darted up the steps. He could hear the sobbing breath.

'Well, you *are* in a hurry, Miss Whitaker,' he remarked pleasantly.

She stifled a scream.

'Oh, Mr. Seal! How you startled me! Yes, I am rather in a hurry, if you'll excuse me please.'

'I'm afraid it's too late, my dear.' He felt he had to warn her. 'She discovered your absence this evening, and she wasn't exactly pleased about it. I thought you might like to know. She's in a damned unpleasant mood,' he laughed.

'Oh!' she said, and wavered thoughtfully. 'It isn't that . . . There's been an accident, or — perhaps you'd come and see. Or — wait! If you'd go and stay there while I went for the — the police and the doctor . . . Could you do that?'

'We-ell . . . Could you be a little more explicit?'

'Listen. Do you know where the old bathing hut is? No? Well, when you get to the bottom of the steps, turn *left* — bear right round the base of the hill and you'll see a little creek at the commencement of Carib Bay. There. You'll see a little hut painted to look like a cottage. Don't let anyone in, Mr. Seal. I'll be back at the earliest possible moment . . . ' She was hurrying down ahead of him as she spoke, for now that she had found him there was no need for her to waste time rousing the others — yet. So she had turned round and started downward again. At the bottom, they separated; Seal in some bewilderment at the way he was being pushed around. And why the police, anyway?

'Here, you'll need this more than I shall, I expect,' she said, and abruptly thrust into his hand a slim torch.

Mr. Seal wandered over the rocks in the direction of Carib Bay.

Ah, here was the hut! The kindly moon flattered its crude colours and blistered paint, faded now by sun and wind. It stood at the edge of a roughly made path facing the sea. The open doorway was a square of blackness inviting him to enter. It was very quiet. He moved forward cautiously.

The narrow beam of light pierced the darkness and slid inquisitively over the rough wooden walls, jerked and wavered, and finally came to rest on the still figure lying prone on the shabby chintz-covered bunk.

It was not necessary for him to touch it or to go any nearer in order to see whether it was alive or dead. There was a flaunting obscenity about the object glinting with such horrible rigidity in the centre of its back, rather to the left of the spinal column, that conveyed the truth at once.

Strange to think he had been inventing murders all these years, and yet this was the first time he had come up against the grotesque reality. He touched one outspread hand gently: it was cold but limp. No mistake about that.

No mistake either about who it was lying there. The golden hair was tousled now, but the brown skin and slim figure were unmistakable. But why on earth was he wearing a lavender silk shirt, violet socks braced with crimson satin suspenders, and *nothing else*?

He swung the torch round the hut. On the floor, as if thrown at random, lay a pair of flannel trousers in a crumpled heap, beside a pair of rubber-soled buckskin shoes. The cushion from the bunk-head lay not far away.

There was not much blood, considering all things. A dark patch stiffening the shirt about the little shining dagger; and a few splashes, he discovered, speckling the wall above the bunk, just below the open window.

He heard a car draw up, and looking out, saw three figures clambering towards him. The police, he surmised

'*Qui est-ce? Qui est-ce?*' called one of them in a richly vibrant voice, and swung a lantern high. Quentin, not understanding, made no reply.

'*Qui êtes-vous, Monsieur?*' challenged the other again at closer range. '*Gendarmes, nous. Brigadier Napoleon Orage, moi.*' He bowed.

'Seal,' murmured Quentin, faint with astonishment, staring at the immense coal-black figure, like an apparition out of a child's story book.

He swung the lantern to and fro above his head and glanced round. One of the constables behind him, a coffee-coloured mulatto man, took out a notebook and pencil and commenced scribbling.

'*Un assassinat!*' commented Brigadier Orage. 'The son of M'sieur Jacques, *hein?*' He knelt down by the bunk and, without disturbing anything, began measuring the position of the body and calling out the results to the constable.

'I am assured you touched nothing, Mr. Seal?'

'It's just as it was when I came in; but don't forget that I wasn't the first person here after the crime. Miss Whitaker was.'

'I ain't forgetting.' He squatted back on

his heels and gazed up at him. 'Are you the Seal who writes the *romans policier*? Gracious to goodness! You heard that, boys? It certainly is a privilege to get acquainted with *you*, sir. Believe I read all you wrote. I learnt from those books most of what I know, if you'll believe me.'

'Oh, they're only written to amuse,' said Quentin, smiling.

'No, sir. They instruct as well as entertain,' he said absently, staring at the heaped clothes on the floor with a puzzled frown. He scrutinised the shoe-soles through a magnifying glass and measured one against the dead boy's foot.

'What do you think he was doing, if it's not a rude question? Going for a midnight bathe?'

'Guess not. No swimsuit anywhere. No towel. Does not seem very likely he was going swimming. I have a little thought somewhere I am trying to catch . . . ' He screwed up his eyes. 'Door was open when you come in, you say? Mind yourself, *Gendarme*.' Without using his hands, he edged the door forward with the toe of his yellow boot. 'Lookit,' he said. 'No handle. Nothing but a keyhole. How's anyone going to fasten a door like that, eh, Marcel?'

The constable grinned and stepped forward in a businesslike manner to dust the door for fingerprints, the apparatus for which he bore in a neat canvas holdall. To facilitate operations, the brigadier stepped outside and inched up and down, peering at the ground hopefully. In a few minutes he stuck his head in at the window.

'Window open like this?'

'Sure,' said Quentin. 'Have you noticed the bloodstains on the wall?'

But just then the doctor arrived, bustling, and pretending to be less shocked than he was. Seal joined the brigadier outside in order to make more room for the doctor. Marcel padded up to tell them there were no prints on the door clear enough or recent enough to use.

'How did they get in and out, for goodness' sake? Were they wearing gloves?'

'Maybe they used the key as a handle — see what I mean? — and the last person out took the key with him, for some reason,' suggested Seal.

'*Merci*,' acknowledged the brigadier. 'Where's that miss got to now? I told her to come back.'

'She went on up to tell the folks,' called the doctor. 'Someone had to break it to them, and thank God it wasn't me, for once. What a tragic family they are; and now, twice in less than a month . . . it's terrible. And who on earth would want to kill a kid like this? For it's murder all right, no doubt about that.'

The doctor joined them.

'Horrible business!' he went on. 'The weapon was a stiletto with a thin pointed blade. It drove under the shoulder blade with a clean downward stroke, and by some extraordinary miracle missed the ribs. If that was not a fluke, it was the most uncanny judgment . . . What's that . . . ? Oh, two hours ago, as near as I care to say. From the attitude of the body and the apparent accuracy of the thrust, I should say that death must have been instantaneous. What's the time now? Eleven-thirty. Say between half-past nine and ten. Later, when I have concluded my examination at the mortuary, I shall be able to tell you more, I expect . . . From where was the blow struck . . . ? That's your pigeon, my dear brigadier. As I was saying, later I shall be able to give you the exact angle at which the blade pierced the vital organ, and you will probably be able to work out from that just where the murderer must have stood. Anything else you want to know? Well, there's nothing more I can do here. If you'll just get your chaps to take the body away, Brigadier — '

The doctor shook hands, and vanished into the darkness after the two gendarmes bearing away the body of the dead youth. A small sad silence lingered after them. Then Napoleon pulled himself together and returned to the hut to examine the bloodstains on the wall.

'Wish I could work out what he was doing here in the dark. How come they killed him? Was he standing like so alongside the bunk, and just fell forward on his face? Or was he lying asleep? Or how? Looks to me like whoever it was done it, was looking for something pretty bad that he must have hoped this fellow had. So, after he kills him, he feels around, see? Looks in the shoes, runs through the pants — no, it ain't there — so he toss 'em down, tries the cushion, too, maybe . . . Well, we don't know what luck he had in the end. Maybe he found it, maybe he was scared away first.'

'It's an idea, anyway.'

Jacques, wild-eyed and haggard, stumbled into the hut, followed by the weary Miss Whitaker. She had tried to stop him, she explained, but in vain, so she had come with him. Where was his boy? he demanded pitifully, and almost wept when they said they had taken him away to the mortuary.

'*Murdered*, you say. Who would have murdered him? Why should anyone — ? And why here?' He stared incredulously at the sordid little hut. He sat with bowed shoulders and head on the edge of the bunk, not speaking, gathering his resources. 'Thank God his mother never lived to see this day,' he said bitterly at last.

'Sir, pardon me, but when did you last see your son?'

He looked up, frowning.

'When . . . ? This evening. Yes. I asked him what he was going to do this evening. And he said he was going to study — stay in his room all evening and study,' he repeated slowly.

'Was he in the habit of coming down to this hut here?'

'So far as I know, he never came down nowadays. It has not been used for five years or more. We frequented it quite a lot before my wife — But recently, not at all. It was always kept padlocked.'

'Is that so? And the key?'

'I wouldn't know. We had one, but goodness knows where it's got to now, and we gave the other to my sister-in-law, I remember.'

'Well, sir, I won't trouble you no more tonight in your grievous affliction.'

'Good Lord, you're not going home to sleep, just like that, surely? A foul crime has been committed; you can't stop working just because your shift is ended,' Jacques expostulated.

'Sir, I ain't stopping work. I got to get in my report yet, and it's almost midnight. There is a lot of routine work to be done yet, sir. Reckon Napoleon Orage won't rest till the murderer is discovered and your son's death avenged.'

A pause to allow it to sink in, and then he added that he would seal up the hut if they would all be so good as to step outside. His moment of triumph was spoiled, however, by the discovery that he had omitted to bring the seals with him, and would be obliged to go all the way back to the station to fetch them. The others agreed somewhat gloomily to remain until he got back.

'Do you think that man will ever be able to solve this, Mr. Seal?' said Prudence.

'Depends on how complicated it is, I suppose. But he's no fool. The question is, how much experience has he had of this kind of crime? Are there many murders on the Island, Mr. Jacques?'

'Native killings, a good few; but I don't believe there's been a white murder for ten years or more,' he said hopelessly.

'Mr. Seal is by way of being a detective, isn't he?' Prudence insinuated.

'I'm just a writer of detective fiction.'

Jacques raised his head. 'You mean he might undertake this ... ?' he said hopefully to the girl.

'Impossible,' said Quentin hastily. 'There is absolutely no connection between real crime and the fake dramatic stuff I knit up. I know my own limitations. I'm not competent to investigate a real murder.'

'Not *interested*, perhaps,' nagged Prudence.

'Listen, Mr. Seal,' said Jacques. 'Only this evening you were telling me how you threw over a regular job for the sake of adventure. Might not this be adventure, too?'

'It isn't that I don't want to. Only you seem to think I have some special qualifications, when in actual fact I probably have far less than you, who know the people intimately. Besides,' he added weakly, 'I don't suppose your native policeman is likely to jump at the idea, either, of having a white and singularly ignorant collaborator thrust on him.'

Inevitably, he yielded in the end.

Jacques was so eager and pathetic, and so grateful to him when he at length consented. He wanted to start at once, only Quentin urged him to touch nothing until Napoleon returned.

They could at least look outside, Jacques decided, to see if the murderer had left some traces of the route he had taken. Quentin was dubious, but he let them go, while he stood frowning in the middle of the room and wondering just what he had let himself in for. He flicked the torch idly to and fro. The chintz was crumpled where the body had lain, and the light cast little hillocks of shadow here and there. He bent forward. In a fold of chintz at the bunk-head, about where Raoul's face must have been, was a short length of thin black wire, three or four inches long, bent double and twisted.

And at that very moment he heard Jacques crying out: 'Who's there?'

Then Prudence, more faintly, calling: 'No, no.'

He slipped the clue into his pocket, therefore, and hurried out.

They were some twenty or thirty yards

from the hut, running to and fro, Jacques waving the lantern over his head wildly. They were both staring out to sea, from whence could be heard the regular chug-chugging of a boat engine. Jacques ran first this way and that, and Miss Whitaker after him, clawing at his coat.

'What is it?' called Quentin sharply. Jacques swung round excitedly.

'There's someone out there without lights. I was trying to see who it was, but the beam doesn't carry far enough. Can you see?'

They listened to the chugging fade to a rhythmic beat and die away altogether.

'Well, whoever it was, they've gone now,' remarked Miss Whitaker a trifle sulkily. 'You scared them away.'

'What makes you say that?' queried Jacques sharply. 'Do you imagine they were coming in here?'

'I've no idea, but it doesn't seem so unlikely to me.'

'If you think that, why didn't you tell me at the time?'

'I did, I did. Good heavens, I kept on shouting at you to stop.'

'How on earth was I to guess you meant that? I thought . . . ' He hesitated and dried up. 'I'm sorry. Please pay no attention to me, I really scarcely know what I am doing or saying just now.'

Napoleon Orage smoothed the situation by arriving just then. He solemnly affixed the seals on the hut door and temporarily boarded up the window.

'*Bonne nuit, 'Sieurs, 'Dames,*' he said politely, in dismissal.

'I'll walk along with you, if you don't mind,' said Mr. Seal. Having said goodnight to the others and advanced with them to the foot of Jacob's ladder, he had hurried to catch up with the easy swinging strides of the native policeman, in order to sound him out gently about the proposed collaboration.

When they reached the Royal Splendide, he asked him in for a drink. There, in the sagging basket chairs, with tall glasses of rum and lemonade before them, he broached the subject tactfully. Napoleon frowned.

'You wouldn't lose any kudos by it, of course,' Quentin hastened to add.

'Kudos?'

'Kudos — glory.'

'Ah!' Napoleon pulled out a notebook and made an entry in pencil. 'Gracious, I ain't caring about kudos, Mr. Seal. I'd be honoured if you were to join up with me. I've never had a white killing to handle yet.'

'It does seem as though I'm fated to be mixed up with these people. This is the second time I've been on the spot practically at once after the two sudden deaths. But don't start imagining that I had anything to do with it on that account,' Quentin warned him.

'No, sir; besides, La Morte wasn't murdered, was she?' Napoleon lit a stinking *caporal* from a blue packet.

'Why, why, why should anyone want to murder a kid like that? Is anyone trying to get at his father through him, do you think?'

'*Cherchez la femme*,' the brigadier said, blowing out a cloud of smoke.

'Good old French psychology, eh? I'll tell you something. I think I recognised the weapon. I've seen it before, I'm

146

almost certain, on Father Xavier's desk.'

Napoleon raised his eyebrows. 'We've got plenty to worry about, ain't we?'

'And — I almost forgot — a clue that you overlooked.' He held out the bit of wire on the palm of his hand. 'Will you let me keep it for a while? I want to try out an idea with it. You've got plenty to get on with, as you say.'

They ran over the facts again together to fix them firmly in their minds. The door without a key. Where was the key? Was it kept somewhere easily accessible by Raoul? Supposing whoever had taken the key had not, in fact taken it, but left it in the door, who knew how long it would have been before Raoul's body was discovered? Did the murderer, then, want to make sure that Raoul was discovered — reasonably soon? *Cherchez la femme!* That must not be forgotten, either. Where was Miss Whitaker going at that time of night? Had the fact that she had slipped out secretly from her bedroom any connection with the murder? How come that she had found the body in that unfrequented spot? The stiletto . . .

147

Bloodstains on the wall . . . a pair of trousers tossed carelessly on the floor . . . the cushion . . . the little piece of wire . . . Was there any connection, however remote, between his murder and his mother's death? Too early to speculate yet. Collect the facts first, then arrange them, and then finally fill in the gaps.

'Native killings are so simple,' sighed Napoleon. 'Someone gets a little drunk, or someone sees his girl two-timing. Something easy.'

'You think this one was premeditated? I shouldn't have said so, but you may be right. Well, we shall see.'

Napoleon took his leave and went, a dark and magnificent figure, striding down the faintly moonlit dusty path, between the slender knotted palms and the chunky banana trees.

Mr. Seal lay beneath the grubby mosquito netting, staring out into the moonlight thoughtfully.

Miss Whitaker had not gone home with Mr. Jacques after all. They had started up the stairs together, but they had got no further than the first turn when Prudence suddenly stopped with an exclamation of annoyance.

'That man! He's got my torch. I must run after him and get it back. Please go on, Mr. Jacques. I'll catch you up.'

And so, obediently, he had gone on, and never noticed that she had not caught up with him. For when he got to the top there was Hattie, distraught and wondering what had happened, and of course the news had to be broken to her, and of course she was most terribly upset. She broke down in Jacques' arms and he comforted her as best he could. It was so awful, such anguish, to remember that they had both been so angry with him a few hours before . . .

But, after all, Miss Whitaker did not bother to catch Mr. Seal, for she found the torch in her pocket. It must have been there all the time. Fancy! Well, it was a pleasant night for a stroll on the beach. She sat down on the sand, looking out to sea. She was afraid her vigil would be useless, but she did not dare to think of that. It amazed her to find how her heart sank at that thought. Of course she might be mistaken about the whole thing; she hoped so fervently. The lagoon itself was safe enough, so they said, but the sea beyond was shark-infested. The light dancing on the placid water created shadows before her tired eyes, sharp-edged triangular shadows. Little spurts and curls of phosphorescence gleamed here and there ... There! Surely she could see a line cleaving the water, hear a languid splashing sound that was not caused by the waves lapping ...

A figure stood up waist-high in the water and stumbled towards the shore. He pitched forward on his face and lay still.

Prudence stood over him. Now that her anxiety was relieved, her rage surged up furiously, like a mother who slaps her child because it was nearly run over.

'Had a nice swim?' she asked coldly.

He rolled over lazily.

'Hallo, Proo-dance.' He was breathing hard, but did not seem very surprised to see her.

'What were you doing? Trying to commit suicide?'

'I'm terribly out of training, Proo-dance,' he grinned feebly. 'I swam too far, I guess. Thought I'd never make the shore. Lucky!'

'Do you always go swimming with your clothes on?'

'Oh, Proo-dance, I am so tired, so unhappy, please do be kind.'

'Are you going to sleep at the hut tonight?' she said carelessly.

'No.'

'Why not?' she jumped in.

'What is the matter, Proo-dance? I am too tired, that's all. It's quite simple.'

'I see. Then I really needn't have troubled myself to come down and warn you not to go there tonight, because Raoul Jacques was murdered there.' She ignored his exclamation and continued: 'I thought if the police saw a tramp hanging around they'd be only too likely to arrest him. So . . . However, now I'm here, you may as well give me the key. Lord knows when you'll be able to use it again, and they're sure to ask for it.'

He didn't reply; her words had given him an idea. He was sitting up scrabbling about in his wet clothes, slapping his pockets anxiously.

When at last he looked up at her, his skin had a curious livid tone, and his lips trembled.

'My papers — ' he muttered. He looked like a great baby on the verge of tears. 'I must have dropped them in the sea. My God! What will become of me? I was so careful to fasten them in securely before I — I don't see how they could have got loose . . . they were all tied together in an oilskin case . . . Proodance, please turn away while I take off my trousers to make quite certain they have not somehow slipped . . . '

And while Prudence stood dazedly with her back to him, the words repeated insanely in her brain. For had there not been someone else just a few hours earlier who also had removed his trousers . . . and met his death like that? Was it no more than a coincidence?

'No,' came his despairing voice, rousing her from her own nightmare. 'Nothing. You may turn round no . . . Here's the key.' He sat down again disconsolately.

'What papers are they?'

'But everything! Passport, identity cards, permits. I might as well not have struggled to reach the land just now. Better if I had not,' he groaned.

'That's ridiculous, Boris.'

'I actually cannot live without them. I cannot move from one place to another, I may not take work, I dare not even be questioned by the authorities now. My situation is hopeless, I tell you.'

'But you've only to report their loss, and the various authorities will look up the details and replace them at once — or pretty soon, anyway.'

'When one has money, when one has a genuine identity, it is all so very simple. But for me it is as good as kaput. It has taken me many years and much patience to acquire those papers, and now they are gone. It is a catastrophe! For one thing, my identity card had not been stamped for seven months. I needed four hundred and twenty francs to get it made up to date. Where am I to get such sums? My passport was a Nansen one; I have no citizenship. And do you think it is easy to get a labour permit — for *anywhere* in the world?'

She could not but feel sorry for him in his desperate plight.

'Don't worry about it anymore tonight. Tomorrow we may be able to think of a solution. You're exhausted now and need some sleep.' She fumbled in her pocket and drew out two limp strips of paper which she handed to him. 'Twenty francs,' she said. 'It's all I have on me, but it will get you a bed and some food. Tomorrow we'll see.'

'Ah, Proo-dance, you are kind and lovely. I shall never be able to repay you.'

'It's a gift, don't worry, not a loan.'

He struggled to his feet. 'No shoes, no papers, I really do look a hopeless tramp now, as you said.'

'It really wasn't worth it, was it?'

'What?'

'Whatever it was that you were doing, that you are too ashamed to tell me about,' said Prudence, and walked away.

8

Preliminary Investigation

'Did you locate the key, Miss Whitaker?' asked Mr. Seal, the next day.

'Yes, knowing you'd want to see it, I looked it out for you.' She held out to him a key-ring containing a large bunch of keys of assorted sizes and shapes. She indicated one of them.

'It was always kept on here.'

'Have you any idea who used it last?'

She shook her head.

'Didn't you use it fairly recently?' he asked.

'I? Oh, no. I know nothing about it. I don't believe I've ever been inside the place, even.'

'Would you mind telling me just how you came to find the deceased?' He changed the subject solemnly. 'I would like to know first of all where you had been and where you were coming from.

You had given Miss Brown to understand that you were not feeling well and had retired to bed. But you crept out secretly, and I would like to know why, and whether you were in the habit of doing so.'

'It's slightly ridiculous,' she assured him with a faint sneer, 'and very unimportant. Miss Brown is so absurdly dominating that she allows me practically no freedom whatsoever. If I insist on going out, then she wants to know all the whys and wherefores. It isn't much fun. It's so much simpler and more pleasant, just to slip away without an argument. I have done that once or twice. But the other night, I did have a headache, and I didn't feel like supper; I just wanted to be quiet. Then, later on, I thought perhaps a little air would do me good once the sun had set. But I didn't want *her* to know and raise a hue and cry, so I kept the door locked and went out of the window — like a schoolgirl. It's idiotic, isn't it?' she added. 'I was strolling about for an hour or more, and I lost all track of time.'

'Have you any idea where you went?'

'I guess I must have wandered about pretty freely. I'm not sure just *where* I went,' she said cautiously.

'Still, you must have *some* idea of where you were coming from when you decided to return. Was it from Wigtown way?'

'No, I was coming from the Bay. And as I passed the hut I saw the door was open. I knew it was always kept padlocked, and so naturally I went to investigate; it seemed my duty.'

'Just a minute. Did you notice whether there was a key in the door?'

'I did. There was not . . . Then I saw Raoul . . . Wasn't it dreadful? I saw at once that there was nothing I could do, and so I was careful not to touch anything. I came away at once.'

'Intending to fetch the police?'

'Yes. Er — that is to say, I thought I ought to tell the family first of all and then go for the police,' she corrected herself.

'I see. And then you met me and changed your mind, is that it . . . ? I was

157

quite wrong, then, in thinking that your object was to get back and into your room unseen, leaving the corpse to be discovered by somebody else in the course of time?'

She went quite pale with anger.

'How dare you! That's insulting, and utterly untrue. I think you owe me an apology for that.'

'Oh, you mustn't be hard on me, Miss Whitaker. I shall have to say much worse than that to you, I'm sure, but I hope you're not going to think it unfriendly of me. After all, this poor young lad . . . Truth . . . and Justice . . . ' he murmured soothingly. 'And there is so much that is odd, that doesn't fit together. The key, now. You say you never used the hut, and that it was always kept padlocked — and yet out of a large bunch of other keys you are able to identify it unhesitatingly. Odd that you should so positively recognise a key you've never had occasion to use. Or is it?'

She shrugged sulkily.

'It's strange,' he said conversationally, 'how one's most innocent and private acts become suddenly of the greatest importance . . . as in this instance. I dare say your little promenades were of the most harmless sort, and yet here I am forced to ask you for the smallest and most intimate details. Of course it's annoying for you, particularly for one of a reserved temperament. I do sympathise, believe me. It is additionally complicated because Raoul too had a very secretive nature, didn't he?'

'Very.'

'What did you think of him?'

'Frankly, and I hope without prejudice, not much. Oh, he was all right, but he was frightfully conceited, and so — French.'

Mr. Seal looked at her quizzically.

'Did he make a nuisance of himself?'

'Yes. But I'm quite capable of handling a kid of that age,' she said primly. 'I never let him get too tiresome.'

'Was he in love with you? Did he ever tell you he loved you?'

'Of course he wasn't. He told every woman he met that he loved her. It didn't mean a thing. He was the last person to want you to believe it, too. That's what I mean — he was French. Compared with an English boy of his age, he seemed depraved. I don't suppose he actually did anything, if you know what I mean, but it was his outlook . . . Mind you, he could be very charming, too — when it didn't cost him anything.'

'Do you think he was in love with anyone? Do you know of anyone who was in love with him?'

'I'm afraid I didn't pay him that much attention. He carried on disgustingly with his aunt, that's all I know, but whether it had any significance I wouldn't know.'

'You don't approve of your employer, do you, Miss Whitaker?'

She hesitated, then:

'Don't trust her, Mr. Seal. You can't believe a word she says, for one thing, and she's really malevolent, a wicked old woman.'

'Proof? Or intuition?' said Mr. Seal.

'Proof. Ask me no more, please,' she begged.

'Very well, we'll leave that for the moment,' he said agreeably. 'When did you say you were last in the hut?'

'Why — er — that would be last night, wouldn't it . . . ?'

'Were you not there *before* Raoul was killed?'

'No, of course not. What makes you think that?'

'Yet this little trademark could only have been left before he was killed.'

He held out his hand, in the palm of which reposed the screw of black wire.

'Is that yours?'

'Of course not.' She laughed scornfully. 'How can you be so stupid? Would I be likely to use a thing *that* colour? It's proof in itself. Don't you see?'

If he was crestfallen, he did not show it.

'Why do you think he was killed? Who do you think did it?'

'I — I don't know. How should I?' She looked at him helplessly.

He rose to his feet. He could hardly expect to get any more information from her just now. He walked away thoughtfully.

He leant over the ramparts and stared down to where the roof of the hut could just be seen round the farthest curve. He was convinced that Prudence knew far more about the key than she admitted; but whether it had anything to do with his particular business was another matter. He did not forget that there was a second key somewhere about that had yet to be found. Well, it was Napoleon's job to find that. Division of labour, and so forth.

The old lady waddled towards him. The stains on her dirty black frock showed up in the strong sunlight. Her hair was in disarray. She looked a mess, as though she hadn't slept all night.

'Ah, I was looking for your brother-in-law . . .'

'He's still in his room. We persuaded him to rest . . . He is not at all well — the shock. And his supply of insulin is running low — that makes him feel ill, too. Don't bother him too much, will you?'

'I'll do my best,' he promised. 'When you last saw your nephew, Miss Brown, do you recall what he was wearing?'

Hattie, her face still smudged and

swollen with tears, screwed up her eyes thoughtfully.

'Navy shorts, I believe, and a pale blue open-neck sports shirt and no tie.'

'Shoes?'

'Either sandals or plimsolls, I suppose. I'm afraid I wasn't paying much attention.'

'Ah, yes, there was some little argument, wasn't there?' said Mr. Seal suavely.

'Nothing to do with the murder, my amateur friend; you needn't waste your time over that.'

'My dear Miss Brown, I hope you're not going to imagine that everything I want to know about I believe to be the source of the murder, or we *shall* have a difficult time. My job is solely to collect as many facts as I can, from which we hope finally to get some sort of picture of the situation. Of course I am only an amateur, you're quite right; so I shall need every one to be specially kind and helpful, won't I?

'The clothes, now. Trivial, perhaps, and yet it suggests things, you know. For instance, although he told his father that he intended to study all evening in his room, he bothered to change his clothes into a silk shirt, buckskin shoes and immaculate flannels. Does one do that in order to study quietly in one's room?'

'There's no way of knowing what men will do; they're crazier than foxes,' said Miss Brown.

'All right, don't help. But it might mean that he lied, that he had an appointment for that night. Or the thought of going out may only have occurred to him afterwards. Or — well, I'm boring you. You were going to tell me what your little quarrel was about.'

'Was I?' She grinned at him in stubborn silence.

'Never mind. You were generally on the best of terms with him, weren't you? Had rather a soft spot for him? I expect you feel his death pretty badly.'

'Of course I do, you fool. But I'd hardly be likely to tell you even if I didn't.'

'Ah, yes, naturally it was a shock. You'd seen him — how long before?'

'Before what? I last saw him just before you arrived.'

'Yes, of course it was a horrible shock for you. I'm so sorry. You can't have thought he had an enemy in the world.'

'I suppose we all think we have no enemies,' said the old woman pensively. 'But probably among our friends and relations there are many who harbour the most venomous hatreds against us. One would imagine that a youngster like that would be loved by all, and yet when one comes to inquire closely into the situation, one might find . . . Well, don't be surprised at what you may discover, Mr. Seal, that's all.'

'That had occurred to me already,' he assured her. 'Don't you remember last night? No, I mean beforehand. Mr. Jacques was enumerating the people who were — annoyed with Raoul. There was the priest, you remember; and Mr. Foley; and Mr. Jacques himself said that he'd like to kill him. Of course, I know he didn't mean it. I don't suppose he meant anything more by it than you did when you threatened to get even with Raoul, earlier. I just mention it in passing, but please don't think that I attach undue importance to it. In the heat of the moment one is quite liable to think — and do, even — things which one would not normally contemplate.'

'How do you know that I said I would get even with him?' asked the old woman quietly.

'I overheard you, Miss Brown. You were quite excited, remember, and your voice was raised.'

'Ah, Mr. Seal, we don't want you to be led on a wild-goose chase. It was nothing much really, though it seemed important to me. When you asked me just now, I felt so upset to think that my last words to him were so embittered that I felt too ashamed to talk about it. You see, it was all because of Omar. You mustn't think me sentimental. Omar was not even a year old, and he did not mean to me what Pierrette does, for instance. But he was superb. He was going to be a king among cats, a perfect breeding tom. And that silly, spiteful little boy killed him.' She flushed. 'I'm sorry. It enrages me even to think about it, you see. It was so pointless, such a nonsensical thing to have done. Can you blame me for being; angry when I found him dead — or dying, rather — and Raoul there, watching him with that expression little boys wear when they pull wings off flies?'

'I can appreciate your feelings. You were in no doubt that he was responsible?'

'Who else would have done it? You don't know the peculiar circumstances, and I can't go into them now, but there was no one else who could have done it, honestly. No one else who would have dared. So in spite of his protests, I knew it was that young devil who was responsible. And so, in my sudden anger, I threatened him with something dire and unnameable in the future. I'm hot-tempered, you know, but it dies down at once and I never bear malice.'

He apparently accepted her explanation.

'Now, this Miss Whitaker?' he began.

'Perhaps you think I have a nasty suspicious nature, but I never feel I can quite trust her. She's thoroughly nice. And that never seems quite normal to me. People are either nice because they want something from you or because they have something to conceal. In a world like this, why should anyone be nice naturally? I distrust nice people on principle.'

'And Miss Whitaker is nice, therefore you distrust her.'

'Don't laugh at me, Mr. Seal. To me, all that girlish timidity and innocence is a con trick . . . Men are more easily fooled, I dare say.'

'In this instance I find myself inclined to agree with you, though. These mysterious departures, now. Where does she go? And why?'

'Yes,' agreed the old woman vaguely, 'there's that too, of course. Silly creature!'

'Does she know many people on the Island? Is she friendly with the English population here?'

'Sorry, the fact is that once her hours of duty are over, I neither know nor care what becomes of her. She is free to do what she likes.'

'But if she is free, why all the secrecy?'

'Why, indeed! Are you trying to fix the murder on her?'

'Oh, come, Miss Brown, I hope I'm not so crude as to try and fasten it on anyone. But there are one or two points ... She did find the body, you know. And she hasn't been quite honest with me. She had the opportunity, but how about the motive? Unless she was consumed by thwarted passion for him, and killed him in a frenzy of unrequited love?' He gazed at Miss Brown hopefully. 'She doesn't look the type, I must say.'

'You'll probably find some more satisfactory theory,' she consoled him. 'I wish I could tell you more about her, but I only know what she has chosen to tell me. She had perfectly good references. And it so happened that I wanted to get rid of my very incompetent mulatto secretary at that time, and I thought an English girl would be useful. So she has.'

'How long has she been with you?'

'About five months or so, I think.'

'Thanks.' He yawned. 'So, although you neither like nor trust her, you don't go so far as to think she murdered your nephew. Anyone else? Any pet predilection?'

She grinned. 'You won't catch *me* by putting salt on my tail, young man.'

There was nothing more to be obtained from her just then, and he went in search of Mr. Jacques. Jacques was looking pale and haggard, the circles beneath his eyes darker than ever. He begged Mr. Seal to excuse him for receiving him in his room . . . Anything he could tell Mr. Seal that might help, if there was anything he could do that might hasten the inevitable judgment, Mr. Seal had only to tell him. He was not a rich man, but what money he had was at Mr. Seal's disposal to enable him to bring the murderer to justice.

Mr. Seal modestly begged him not to expect too much from him. *He* could not hope to bring the criminal to book, but he did hope that he might be able to *help* here and there.

These courteous preliminaries concluded, the questioning began. But there was not much that Jacques had to tell that he did not already know. He had been angry with the boy, but so had several other people, and with reason. He never

170

had a chance to tell him so. He had sent him — as he thought — to his-room, intending to rebuke him later, and he had never seen him again. He had no idea that the boy used the hut, nor did he know whether he had ever had occasion to use it before since it was shut up. As for where and when he had got hold of the key, that too was a mystery to him, for he could not recall where the key was kept. One he had given to Miss Brown, yes, but the other one . . . ?

And then suddenly, in the middle of some other question, he remembered that Julia had kept the key in her desk, in the secret drawer, in the little purse where she kept the money. He looked at Seal anxiously. What did that signify? he wondered.

So, whoever had access to the purse had access also to the key. That narrowed it considerably. For instance, the nurse, suspected by so many, had left some time ago, so she could hardly be involved in this business.

She might not have left the Island, Jacques reminded him . . . Great heavens, why had it not occurred to them before? Didn't Mr. Seal see? She could easily have taken the key — deliberately. She was furious at being accused of the theft, one had to bear in mind. Supposing she meant to revenge herself somehow, someday? She waits for the fuss to die down, and then — perhaps she writes a note to Raoul inveigling him down to the hut on some pretext or another. Then she goes down there. Perhaps they have an argument, perhaps she just stabs him in the back without warning. She hurries away again, and more than likely steps straight on to the first boat she sees ready to leave the Island. She might be almost anywhere now.

'Not *anywhere*. One can't get very far in twelve hours. It's a good start, but it doesn't mean that she is utterly beyond recall — if we find that she really is the guilty person,' said Mr. Seal.

'You don't think that is a correct analysis?'

'I've heard stupider theories. The first thing is to find out whether she left the Island after the inquest or not. I'll put

Brigadier Orage on to that little job; that's more in his line than in mine.'

After a few more questions, he left Jacques and went in search of Napoleon and his gendarmes. He found them seated about the dining-room table, taking down Prudence's report of what had happened. He came in just as she was telling them as accurately as she could what had transpired when she broke the news to Jacques of his son's death.

' . . . and he asked to be taken to him at once. Then he said quickly, 'How did it happen? Is he in pain? Is it serious? Is he conscious?' I implored him to keep calm. I told him he was not in pain, he was not conscious, but it was serious . . . He dropped his head into his hands and began to moan. Then he asked again how it happened, and I didn't answer. And he said, 'Let's go at once.' I said, 'There is no need to hurry now, Mr. Jacques' — or something like that. And he looked at me — for the first time, really — and I saw he understood. He was very upset, naturally. I gave him some brandy and made him sit down for a while. But he insisted on going down to the hut almost at once. So I went with him, and on the way I told him the little more I knew myself.'

That was the end of that. They read it out to her and she signed it. That was the last of the statements. Miss Whitaker was dismissed. Napoleon and Quentin exchanged reports. Then they went to the dead boy's room to see what further illumination awaited them there.

In an impersonal sort of way, the room revealed his personality: a touching blend of the schoolboy and the man-about-town, of immaturity and sophistication. On his dressing-table were expensive toilet preparations, brilliantine, talcum, a smart little flacon of Tweed, jostling more mundane objects like plain wooden-backed hairbrushes.

In the bookcase beside his bed, books on algebra, the elements of the French civil code, and a Latin grammar leant against the sultry covers of *Le Kamasutra* and *Les Chansons de Bilitis*.

In his top drawer, in an unassuming cardboard box, they found a quite remarkable collection of jewellery — remarkable, that is, for a boy of his age. There were some charming gold and enamel links, a slim silver cigarette case with an enigmatically-initialled inscription inside, a very *sportif* platinum watch-bracelet, besides other smaller pieces of dubious taste.

There was some enviable silk under-wear, too, among the deceptive piles of cotton and mercerised. At the very back of the drawer was a striped silk purse which seemed somehow familiar to Quentin. Then he realised that he had not seen it before, but had recognised it from, the description of the stolen purse belonging to Julia Jacques. So that was where it had got to. And that was how Raoul had come by the key. That was useful to know. It told them *he* had the key; therefore, the murderer had either gone there to meet him or had surprised him there. But if the murderer had not had the key in the first place, was it the murderer who had taken it afterwards? Or was it someone else? Unless Prudence had taken it in order to hide the loss of the other key, the one that should have been in her possession? But why should she have done that? Unless she knew, or thought she knew, who . . . In that case, perhaps she had taken it in the belief that she was shielding someone that way. Seal opened another drawer.

Here he came across the most fantastic trophies. A sort of album-diary in which were pasted letters and notes from his various girlfriends — apparently in chronological order, though undated — and his own comments and descriptions, hovering between the lurid and the sentimental; and adorned by photos, sometimes artful studio portraits, sometimes an almost indecipherable snapshot. It was evidently a kind of insurance against the boredom and forgetfulness of old age, to enable him to review his past triumphs and reheat the thinning blood with the glow of memory. The absurdity of it, the careful pride of this young Lothario, made Quentin smile.

And there was an innocent-looking notebook in which he kept the most staggering accounts. Under initialled headings which discreetly hid the identities of his objectified passions, was carefully tabulated every penny he had spent on them directly and indirectly. And against this was balanced everything they could be presumed to have spent on him. It was an incredible document. Here was computed not only the cost of his presents, including the various pieces of jewellery above-mentioned and so on, but on every kiss and embrace he had fixed a precise valuation as though they were from venal women. It was in fact a veritable tariff of love. To Quentin, there was something horrifying about the mind that conceived of love entirely in methodical business terms.

9

Pussy Passed By and She Looked In

Palm Point was Quentin's next port of call. Mrs. Foley was in and would see him. She greeted him brightly, but it seemed to him that she looked fatigued, with smudges of weariness beneath her eyes and her purple-stained lids heavier than ever. She was wearing flowered chiffon pyjamas, loose and fluttery.

An native servant brought drinks. He was middle-aged and had a sly expression. Albert, his name was; which Mrs. Foley's French accent pronounced *Ulbear*.

'Ulbear will make the drinks,' she said, throwing herself languidly into a wicker-and-bamboo long-chair. 'He's very good at it. He's had a lot of experience, haven't you, Ulbear?' she added bitterly.

Quentin waited discreetly for Albert to take himself off. And then murmured reverently that she knew of course why he had come.

'To see me, I should hope,' she said vivaciously.

'You mean, you haven't heard yet?'

'I must be out of the circuit. What's happened?'

'I'm sorry to bear evil tidings,' said Quentin. 'It's young Jacques. He was killed last night.'

She stared at him. Her mouth opened and closed again wordlessly, and her tongue flickered over her lips. And then without warning her face crumpled up like a rag and she hid it in her hands.

He thought she was shamming at first till he saw tears trickle through her fingers.

'Oh, my God! It's too terrible! Killed. It doesn't seem possible,' After a while she raised her head. 'It was an awful shock . . . to think of him . . . so young . . . I couldn't help crying. It's all terribly cruel and unnecessary.' She dabbed her eyes. 'There! I'm all right again. Please give me a cigarette and tell me how it happened.'

'I wish we knew,' he prevaricated, as he obediently held a flame to her cigarette. 'At present it is something of a mystery. I suppose you didn't happen to see him at any time last night?'

'Heavens, it's ages since I saw him last. Can't remember when. When Johnny made all that fuss, I suppose. But you were there, you must remember it too. No, as a matter of fact, I didn't go out at all last night. I went to bed directly after supper. I was tired. And to think of that poor kid! How was he — ?'

'He was stabbed in the back,' he said, 'and — '

'Murdered!' she cried, and her hands flew up to her mouth. 'Do you mean *murdered?*'

'Must have been. He can hardly have stabbed himself in the back, can he?'

'But *who* would have done — ?'

'Ah, that is what we are trying to find out. I'm hoping you'll be able to help me.'

'Me? I'll do anything I can, of course, but I know nothing. I can't bear to think of it, even.'

'You won't think me unsympathetic,

Mrs. Foley, but it has got to be thought of — by somebody, if we are to bring the assassin to justice. Besides, he was a friend of yours, wasn't he?'

'I took a motherly interest in him,' she admitted guardedly.

'I dare say he confided in you quite a bit? Young boys often confide in mature women, if they can find one tolerant enough to listen . . . He had a peculiar character in some ways,' he mused, and began forthwith to tell her about the curious albums found in Raoul's room. He managed to convey a good deal without saying much. And she didn't like any of it — that was plain to see, though she tried to disguise it.

'I'm afraid you've disillusioned me,' she said with a wry smile, shaking her head. She got up and began trailing up and down the room restlessly. Something fell to the ground with a faint tinkle. Quentin bent to pick it up.

'Yes, but even blackguards must not be murdered, must they? Did he ever suggest to you that he had any enemies?'

'Enemies? A kid like that!'

'All the same, he must have had an enemy. Of course, anything you told me would be in confidence,' said Mr. Seal.

She did not, she said, understand him.

He thought there had been some trouble with Mr. Foley over Raoul. Had not Mr. Foley forbidden her to see him again? If Mrs. Foley had — for one reason or another — met Raoul again, there was no reason why it should not come to Mr. Foley's knowledge.

'But you are quite mistaken, Mr. Seal. I have already told you that I did not see him. I had a headache last night and went to bed early.' She smiled patiently.

'What time did Mr. Foley get in last night, do you know?'

She shook her head. 'I was asleep.'

'Sleeping the sleep of the just,' he said genially. He held out his hand. 'You just dropped this.'

She took the pin absently and replaced it.

'He must have been back pretty late,' he said, 'because it was well after ten when he arrived at Miss Brown's.'

She paused suddenly in her restless

promenade and stared at him. 'Were you there?'

'Oh, yes, I was there all right. By the way. Mrs. Foley. I gave you the wrong pin just now. Would you mind giving it back to me . . . No, you put it this side. Sorry to be so insistent over something so trivial. Thank you.' He held the two little twists of wire out on his hand side by side. 'You see how similar they are? Hardly possible to distinguish which is which, is it? But this one . . . ' He tapped the edge of it lightly with one finger. ' . . . this one was found — in the hut. You understand me?'

She gazed at him wide-eyed. 'No! What am I supposed to understand? What has it to do with me?' She added defiantly: 'I've told you twice I wasn't there.'

'And I,' he said amiably, 'am suggesting that you are mistaken. How else could you have understood the significance of my remark otherwise? Logic, Mrs. Foley. If you had not been to the hut, if it was not your hairpin that was found there, how was it that you knew what I meant, *although I had not told you and you had not asked where the murder took place.* It was not necessary — because you *knew.*'

She said nothing. She sat down abruptly, gazing out of the open window to where the distant sugar-cane plantations shimmered in the heat.

Mr. Seal admired the little black twists of wire and his own cleverness. Black hairpins for black hair, hairpins that slid too easily from the soft waves, such slender pieces to make a trap with, and yet he had brought it off. How delightful!

She turned wearily. 'What are you going to do?'

'Listen to what you have to say, first of all.'

'You mustn't imagine that I know anything about this ghastly murder, just because I lied to you about having been down there.'

'Suppose you tell me all about it before we make any decisions,' Quentin said gently.

She twisted her slim white fingers together.

'He kept writing such pathetic notes, you know, after Johnny forbade him to come to the house again. He begged me to meet him just *once*. He was so insistent I hadn't the heart to refuse. I may have wanted to get my own back on Johnny a little, too, No woman would stand being made a fool of like that; he's too absurdly jealous. Not that I intended any mischief, only I didn't care to be treated as a bauble to be shut up in a glass case and taken out to exhibit to visitors. Besides, if Johnny was right and Raoul was beginning to imagine himself in love with me — well, what woman could resist the temptation to find out for herself? Especially when her mirror tells her daily that romance is over for her.' She cast up her heavy lids in an appealing glance . . . Mr. Seal coughed deprecatingly . . . 'Not that I took that kiss to mean anything. I honestly didn't see how he could be in love with me,' she assured him earnestly. 'I thought it must be about something quite different that he wished to see me.'

She sighed. 'Well, in the end, I agreed to meet him just once more and to listen to what he had to say. I wish to God now that I had not. The bathing-hut was his suggestion, because it was never used and we were unlikely to be seen.'

She got up, poured vermouth and gin and the remains of the ice into the shaker, and agitated it.

'I went,' she resumed, 'and listened to what he had to say, and then I came away. That was before the murder.'

'So he stayed there alone and waited to be murdered.'

She shrugged. 'I don't know anything about that.'

'What time was it when you met him — and when you left? Do you know that at least?'

'I don't know why you should take that tone with me; I'm trying to be helpful. I was supposed to meet him there at nine o'clock, and I remember hearing the church clock strike while I was on the way. And I left — oh, say, half-past at the latest. I was home soon after ten.'

'Well, the servants can verify that, I daresay.'

She moistened her lips.

'No,' she said. 'As it happens, they had

the evening off, and they don't sleep in, you see.'

He watched her pouring the iced liquid.

'Now, I wonder whether that is convenient or inconvenient for you. I can't help thinking it's rather unlucky that there is no one — alive — to verify your story,'

'Don't you believe me?'

'There's the business of this maddening little hairpin, you see,' he said apologetically.

She brought the full glass across to him with a steady hand.

'Thank you. Don't you want to know where it was found? It was found *beneath* his body — or, rather, his head, on the bunk on which he was lying.'

'Quite so. Is there any reason why it should not have dropped out of my hair as I sat there? One fell out just now, didn't it?'

He had to admit the truth of that. He hesitated, then:

'On the face of it, I can't think why you bothered to lie in the first place, since there was so little to it.'

'If it had not been for the hairpin, you would never have known I was there at all. It was not a thing I cared to broadcast; I'm sure you can see that. It's pretty asinine for a woman of my age to run after a boy, isn't it?'

'But it was he who ran after you, you said.'

'How many people would accept my version of it, do you suppose? And it's not only a question of my pride, but my husband's. It's one thing to make a fool of him to myself, and quite another to make a public laughing-stock of him. I'm devoted to John, I wouldn't hurt his feelings for the world.'

He rose to his feet.

'You've been very patient, Mrs. Foley. I won't keep you any longer. By the way, during this last interview, was the door of the hut kept open or shut?'

'It was closed,' she decided, pondering. 'On account of the privacy.'

'And when you left, what happened?'

A look of uneasiness crossed her face, 'Now, let me see ... He came and unlocked it and let me out, I suppose.'

'And what did he do afterwards? Did he lock himself in again? Or leave it open behind you? Or did he follow you out and lock it behind him . . . or what?'

'Why do you look at me like that? I tell you, I don't know. I wasn't paying attention. I wasn't to know he was going to be killed directly afterwards, was I? I said good-bye and went away and thought no more about it.' Her voice rose a little shrilly.

'He never mentioned to you whether he was going back home or somewhere else, or even whether he had another assignation there that night? Perhaps he had a premonition of his impending doom and was going to say farewell to all his lady-friends, one after the other,' he suggested.

'I think that remark is in the worst possible taste.'

'A trifle crude,' he admitted, 'but then so was its subject. All right. Objection sustained. He didn't offer to see you home?'

'No . . . Have you forgotten that it

189

suited neither of us to be seen together?' she added testily.

'Quite so. Then you knew he was remaining behind, and when I told you he was dead you at once jumped to the conclusion that he had been murdered at the hut. But of course you knew nothing about it until I mentioned it. Well, well, well, we shall doubtless meet again.'

He bowed graciously and departed.

Her story rang so false that it was impossible to gauge where the truth lay, but on the other hand it was useless to persist with her just then — for, found out in one lie, she merely proffered another, and one was no better off than before.

Still, he had found out that she had been there after all, and without doubt she knew more about it than she pretended. A clever actress with excellent control over her limbs and features, but not able to evade subtle traps.

Though a pathological liar, she seemed less awkward to deal with than the others he had examined so far. That Miss Brown, now, she was a tricky one. And as for Prudence, either she had nothing to hide, or she was far more subtle than one would believe from her general attitude.

From the plantations came a rhythmic chant, a monotonous but quite pleasant song with mournful harmonies. The words were inaudible, but he caught glimpses of the natives dipping and bending at their work.

10

The Police Make an Arrest

He handed over his information to the brigadier, who smiled entrancingly — especially at the part about the hairpin and its deceitful owner.

Nor had *he* been idle, and he had plenty to share with his new colleague. He had been to see the good Father Xavier, who had identified the stiletto as his paper-cutter. He had emphatically denied ever using it for any other purpose, and neither could he say definitely when he had last noticed it in its proper place on the table. After much persuasion, he had finally narrowed it down to the day Raoul came and insulted him. He remembered that he was fidgeting with it nervously as he tried to restrain his natural anger with the boy, and then in the excitement and intensity of emotion he had gripped it unthinkingly in his hand and cut his fingers on the sharp blade. He had showed the healed scars to Napoleon. They were quite slight, he reported, and could have been made by the stiletto just as well as by anything else. The priest could not recall seeing it after Raoul left.

'Meaning to imply that Raoul probably snatched it, eh?' said Mr. Seal.

Napoleon nodded knowingly.

'But of course he *may* have,' said Quentin judiciously. 'We don't want to be too clever.'

'We are in agreement, sir.'

'Napoleon, before we go any further . . . Are you a brave man? How do you feel about a little experiment? It probably won't hurt you, but I'm pretty sure it would kill me if I attempted it. It's like this. I wasn't so very far from the actual site of the murder during the time it was taking place. And I'd seen him only a little while before, when he said that he was going to his room to study all evening. It all actually took place within a few hundred yards of me.

'But this is the point. I was at dinner

with two of the people who had been quarrelling with him just a short while before he was killed. And there was a brief space during that dinner when they left me. Miss Brown went to find Miss Whitaker, but she was not in her room, and so she very likely took longer to search for her than she would otherwise have done. Not only that, but, as she was unable to open Miss Whitaker's door, she went round the outside to try her shutters, which she succeeded in opening because they were not fastened. So far, so good. She thus saw that the bird had flown. I know this because she returned via the courtyard. I remember noticing she was rather pale and panting; I thought at the time it was indignation.

'At about the same time, Mr. Jacques had excused himself in order to fetch me some rather special port he had upstairs. He left after her and returned just before, it's true, so he was away only a short time, but we must remember that he *was* away. However, he returned slowly bearing the port. But let us suppose for the moment that he wangled the port somehow as an alibi. Was there time for him to have gone downstairs, halfway round the base of the mountain to the hut, stabbed the boy, run back, up the stairs, seized the port *en passant* and borne it calmly and steadily into the dining-room? Was it possible? And by the same token, was it possible for the old girl to have done the trip instead of bothering with that Miss Whitaker? That is what we have to consider. And the simplest way is to test the theory by having one of us time the route.' Mr. Seal coughed affectedly.

'I thought, my dear Napoleon, that the most seemly course would be for me to sit on the ramparts with my invaluable stopwatch in my hand, while you execute — in your admirable way — the more physical aspect of the experiment. Does that meet with your approval?'

And less than an hour later they were on the ramparts, with the brigadier stripped for action. Quentin released the catch of his stopwatch and Napoleon started from the shadow of the tower.

Down the steps he skimmed like a

great black bird, and Quentin, by leaning dangerously far over, could see him scrambling over the sea-splashed rocks in the direction of the dilapidated cabin. In, and out again almost at once, re-tracking over the rocks, and then swarming up the first flight of steps, stumbling, saving himself, and on ... to arrive with bursting eyes and lungs and the sweat running in little rivers down his heaving body.

'Twelve and a half minutes,' announced Mr. Seal. 'And I bet that's the record for the course. I didn't mean you to kill yourself entirely, my poor fellow. Well, twelve and a half, and neither that heavy old woman nor that sick old man could do it in less than fifteen, not without collapsing afterwards. And yet I'm sure that the old girl was not gone for more than ten minutes, and Jacques less than that, of course. So it looks as if they're out, unless she flew down on her broomstick! Thank you, Napoleon, thank you. You've cleared my mind. It's nice to have somebody washed out, even though they were my favourite suspects — at least, she was. We've already killed off our so-called hero, and that's bad enough.'

'What about a motive?'

'All right, then, we'll examine the motives. How about the dear Father, in that case? I confess I'm not altogether satisfied about him. What do you think? La Morte, remember, left him the bulk of her money. Or, rather, she left the money to the Church in his name. So be it. The other side maintained that there was some dirty work involved. His lordship was very discreet and retiring about the whole concern. But let us assume that there was something fishy somewhere.' Quentin rubbed his nose. 'And let us assume that Raoul somehow discovered the fact and tackled the priest with it. What then? *That* might indeed lead to trouble, might it not? *That* would be a motive for his reverence to still that unruly member, Raoul Jacques' tongue. No?'

Napoleon whistled shrilly between his teeth by way of comment.

'That's how I'd make it in a book, anyway,' amended Quentin. 'But reality is a different proposition. Perhaps the main point in its favour is the stiletto. It's just the sort of unthinking, asinine thing people do in real life. It's the sort of thing he'd snatch up without considering. We must also remember that he tried to convey that Raoul had taken it himself. That was rather a funny thing to say, unless — '

As they descended the steps again, they met Antoine Jacques on his way home from the Courts of Justice. They conversed civilly of this and that. And then, just as they were leaving one another, Seal suddenly remarked:

'That reminds me. Do you remember when you were at Father Xavier's the other day — about your son, you know — did you notice whether there was a stiletto on his writing-table?'

'The writing-table,' Jacques frowned. 'One moment, please, gentlemen. I have a very good visual memory . . . ' He leant back against the stone balustrade and closed his eyes. Then: 'No. I could almost swear there was no stiletto there. I can see the table quite plainly. There were a lot of papers on it, and it might just conceivably have been concealed beneath them, but I think not; I think it was not there.'

Quentin threw a meaning glance at the brigadier as they strolled towards the police station. 'Do you see the significance? Oh, this is very interesting indeed. It remains now for Mr. Foley to corroborate that. I wonder if he will.'

It was while they were sitting in the inner office of the police bungalow, the electric fan whirring, that the wire-netted frame-doors swung open cautiously and a head poked in. 'Psst! Brigadier!'

Napoleon looked up irritably at the interrupter, a khaki-clad mulatto man.

'What are you after now, Alphonse? I'm busy,' said the policeman testily.

He sidled up to the table and blinked at them in an indescribably sly manner.

'A little bit of information and evidence, gentlemen. You never can tell when Alphonse is going to be useful — '

'Cut it out,' begged Napoleon curtly. 'Alphonse is a clerk of Miss Brown's,' he explained to Quentin. 'Well, what's it about? What's the evidence relate to?'

'I wouldn't want to waste your valuable time, gentlemen. It may be that poor Alphonse is mistaken after all.' He moved to the door, 'Only thing is, I can't make up my mind whether to hand it to Mr. Jacques or — '

'*Render unto Caesar that which is Caesar's,*' said Napoleon drily. Alphonse, with his hand on the door, turned.

'Fifty francs,' he remarked to the door.

'Nothing doing,' growled Napoleon.

'Forty!'

'Git! You're wasting our time.'

'Gentlemen,' wailed Alphonse, his eyes large with unshed tears, 'gentlemen, I assure you, it is worth every penny of thirty francs. I swear it on the head of my mother.'

'You can leave her out of it.'

'Twenty-five, gentlemen. Positively my last word.'

'Show, or git. I promise nothing, Alphonse.'

Alphonse sighed and reluctantly came back to the table. Out of his khaki shorts, he pulled a rag, and from within the folds of the rag he produced with immense secrecy — a key.

Quentin, taking his cue from his companion, looked at it impassively, though he knew what it was.

'Well?' said Napoleon stolidly.

'Sir, you do not recognise it? This is the unique and inimitable key to the cabin of death.'

'*The cabin of death*, excellent,' said Quentin. 'Did you get that out of the papers? Where did you find it?' Napoleon's heavy sole clamped down on his foot, shutting him up — a little late.

'Twenty-five francs, gentlemen,' he recommenced, and they went through the argument all over again. At last, a trifle weary and dejected, Alphonse gave in.

The key, he had discovered in the course of his duties — so he said — locked in a drawer in Mr. Foley's desk. He maintained that, as Mr. Foley's head clerk, he had access to the entire office and that nothing was private from him. He had duplicate keys for all doors and drawers. He had been looking for some carbon paper, it seemed; and, feeling convinced that there was some in the locked drawer, he opened it — and, lo and behold, what should meet his astounded gaze but this very key! Naturally, his first thought had been to bring it to the police.

'You seem to know a mighty lot about it,' said Napoleon disagreeably. 'How come you're so certain it's the right key?'

Alphonse was offended. He had naturally made certain on that point before he bothered the gentlemen. No, he had been careful not to touch it himself, *he* didn't wish to be guillotined for murder.

It certainly was no office key; he had made sure of that at once. And then, with a magnifying glass, he had seen on the indented neck of the handle little rusty smears of blood . . . or what he took to be blood. Anyway, he had put two and two together. Whether it was the genuine key or not hardly mattered to his scheme of things, providing he could convince the policeman and fool him just long enough to collect the money.

'And who do you think put it there?'

'Sir, I cannot tell who put it there, but only Mr. Foley has the key to the drawer.'

'Not quite true. You also have a key. You could have easily put it there yourself. You quite probably did.'

'No, sir. I did nothing of the kind. I shall not stay here to be insulted. Oblige me by paying me my fee, and I will depart.'

Quentin turned to Napoleon judicially. 'I'm not sure that we ought to let him go. Might it not be wiser to detain him for further questioning? If the other side got hold of him and bribed him, who knows what he might say? Better to keep him here. We have plenty of empty cells.'

That got rid of him. He didn't wait for his 'fee' after that. The others laughed. Then they became serious again and stared at the key thoughtfully.

'It would be interesting to have Mr. Foley down at the station for a little chat. He might have something germane to say on the subject. What do you think?'

And, while Mr. Foley was being snared and brought to the station, they discussed the meaning of Alphonse's evidence.

'I suppose it suits you down to the ground, Napoleon. There you have motive and your beastly *cherchez la femme*, and all the rest of it.'

'You don't buy it?'

'I don't know about that. It has its good points. He had some kind of a reason to commit the crime. He was jealous, his wife admits it quite openly — and so did he, for that matter — and there had been quite a row on the subject, in which finally he forbade Raoul to come to the house, or to see Mrs. Foley again. All this on account of a kiss, so the story goes. Anyway, the pair were forbidden to meet. Whether they did or not, Mr. Foley suspected they were meeting, and even made occasion to mention the fact to Mr. Jacques, imploring him to use his influence with the boy. That much is common knowledge. We know, too, that he went to visit the priest — contrary to his custom, for he apparently regards all priests as popish knaves. And that same evening, Raoul is killed in the bathing-hut, which was customarily kept locked. And Evelyn Foley, who was supposed to be in bed with a headache, was — for a time, at least — in the hut with him. A curious assignation, and an unusual rendezvous, I must say. Now, it would be odd, but scarcely improbable, if Foley discovered this. He might even have seen his wife there. Then, we imagine, his jealous fury got the better of him. He stabbed the unfortunate youth. And then . . . ? Then he resumes his journey up to Castelnuovo, to go over the accounts with Miss Brown as he was bidden. When he arrives, he is dishevelled but not distraught, hot but not heated, anxious but not alarmed. And doubtless in his heart he felt much relieved, as he fastened together the threads of his alibi.'

'You don't like it,' said Napoleon. 'I can tell.'

Quentin's face was disconsolate. He ran his fingers through his hair.

'It's perfectly all right. It all fits together. I dare say it's good enough for real life, but it wouldn't do for a book, that's all. The psychology is wrong. It just doesn't happen to satisfy my fastidious mind. Too bad!'

'Mr. Seal, I'd be obliged if you'd tell me what's troubling you,' said the brigadier patiently.

'If he weren't an Englishman, it would be all right, Napoleon. I can't visualise any Englishman acting that way. *Cherchez la femme*, perhaps, but we shouldn't be hag-ridden. If he had shot him, now, that would be something. But to have stabbed him in the back with a stiletto! It just doesn't ring true to me.'

'You ain't forgetting,' said Napoleon softly, 'it could have been premeditated.'

Quentin stared at him, round-eyed. 'You mean it may have been deliberately done in order to throw suspicion on someone else? No, I never thought of that. You're very likely right. That would explain it very reasonably. You see, Napoleon, he's made such a to-do about his wife and how much he loves her that I never thought for a moment he would do anything. Besides, Englishmen never take their wives as seriously as all that. They marry to get it off their mind, as a rule, and that's that. Of course some of them love their wives, I suppose, in the nature of things, but surely not the ones that make such a shout about it. And in any case, one doesn't murder the other chap, it would be such damned bad form. He might grovel a bit to his wife and cry, that would quite likely be in his line, but murder displays one's private sentiments too openly. In England, the *crime passionnel* is exceedingly rare and indeed is not taken account of by our law.'

At that moment Foley walked in, followed by a gendarme. He was on the verge of giving a display of justifiable indignation, but they calmed, him down with a flow of trivial questions importantly asked. They tested his alibi inch by inch, and he only leant back in his chair smiling, without showing the least perturbation. They travelled backwards through time till they arrived at the priest's house. They fooled about a bit, pretending they wanted to know why he had gone to see the priest, and then insidiously demanded whether he had noticed the paper-cutter on the priest's table.

'Do you mean a sort of thing like a stiletto?' He sketched a shape vaguely in the air. 'Was that what the lad was done in with? I say! Oh, yes, I saw it there all right. Does that mean the priest — ' He whistled, and his eyes went sharply from one to the other.

'Then there's this little business of the key,' said Quentin smoothly. 'I expect you know all about that. Mmm?'

'I don't think so.'

Quentin leant forward.

'The key to the bathing-hut, you know, was missing. It's turned up again, though, by what I suppose one might call a lucky chance. But I'm sure you can explain quite easily. We thought it would simplify things so much if we asked you to come along and explain how the key came to be in a drawer of your office desk.'

He lost colour, but not composure.

'I'm afraid my explanation won't be very helpful — I found the key — in my pocket. I at once put it in my desk for safety — intending to hand it over to you later. I can't tell you how it got into my pocket, I don't know.'

'You hadn't any doubt what the key was for?'

'No. I — I don't think I thought twice about it . . . I seemed to *know* . . . I've

208

seen it in Miss Brown's study often enough . . . '

'Something of a feat to recognise a key you've never used, that you've only seen on a key-ring!'

He shrugged. 'Any further questions? Because if not, I think I'll be going.' He rose to his feet.

Napoleon rose, too. 'I think not,' he said suavely. And the gendarme moved a noiseless step nearer.

'What do you mean?' He went deadly pale and turned to Quentin. 'Good God, Seal, you aren't going to let these fools — You can't think for a moment, that I . . . '

'Your wife has admitted that she was in the cabin with Raoul before he was killed.'

For an instant he said nothing, as though he was letting the words sink in. Then he exclaimed wildly:

'So you've found that out, have you? She admitted it! That's good, that's rich . . . It's a trap! I don't believe a word of it! Take your damned hands off me, you insulting black cur! How dare you touch me!' His eyes blazed wildly. He pulled himself free and crashed through the frame-doors in an attempt to get away. But even that faint breath of liberty seemed to frighten him, and he stood there rubbing his forehead with a bewildered expression.

'I don't know what came over me,' he said. 'It was the shock of it made me go queer for a minute. I'm sorry.' He gave a little broken laugh. 'I'll go quietly.'

When Napoleon returned, he found Quentin with his chair tilted back, looking much more cheerful than before.

'It looks better than it did. I think we may have the wrong motive but the right reasoning. Yes, yes, it may be that . . . What did you think of that pretty little exhibition just now?'

'I reckon he was pretty sore at Missus Foley giving him away like that.'

'Maybe so. Or perhaps he was just sore. Eh? He got control of himself pretty quickly again. I wonder what took the fight out of him so suddenly . . . ?'

11

The Maiden Speaks

It was fearfully hot in the Royal Splendide Hotel, no breeze blew through the narrow dusty streets of Wigtown.

Quentin, staring at the fly-blown brownish ceiling, felt that the case was not yet concluded. There were the holes and there were the pieces, but the one did not fit the other, and no amount of contriving and pushing would make them go right.

A shadow on his veranda, overlooking the main street, made him turn his head. A slight, familiar figure pressed anxiously at the netting before the window, and with a hurried glance behind her, slipped into the room.

'Good heavens, madam, you can't come in here!' exclaimed Mr. Seal, hastily pulling the sheet about bis burly torso.

'I'm sorry, Mr. Seal. But I didn't wish

to be seen by anyone passing outside, you see,' said Prudence.

Mr. Seal swathed his improvised sarong more firmly about him. 'If you touch me I shall call for help, madam.'

'Don't joke, please,' she implored him. 'I had to come.' She moved to the door, opened it just wide enough to see that no one lurked outside, and locked it. Then she turned to the man on the bed and said: 'I'm frightened.'

'So am I,' said Mr. Seal.

She looked anguished.

'How can I make you understand the danger? If she finds out . . . She's a witch. I think she could find out anything if she set her mind to it. Yet what can she do to me if she does find out?' She heaved a great sigh.

'It's Miss Brown again, eh? Come, sit down and make yourself comfortable.'

She pulled off her hat and fanned herself with the brim. She tossed something pink towards him. Its soft irregular lumpiness fell into his out-stretched hand.

'Open it,' she said. He undid the clasp

of the bag and tumbled out the contents onto the bed. A jumble of letters, compact, spectacle case, comb, loose coins, tickets, hairpins — bronze this time, he noted — and an ivory curio . . . no, a doll . . . hello! A little mannikin roughly moulded in wax. He turned it over. A lock of grey hair was fastened to its head. Threads and snippets of rags were tied here and there to its limbs and body, which was scored with pin-like scratches and hieroglyphics,

'Is this what you wanted me to see?' he asked. 'What is it supposed to be?'

'Have you never seen such a thing before? I recognised *that* all right directly I saw it.' She turned her head away. 'It's a spell-poppet.'

He said gravely: 'I've never heard it called that before, but I think I know what you mean. Isn't it a mannikin made to carry out a charm or enchantment?'

She nodded, rather shamefaced.

'You don't believe in those things, do you? Neither did I — but I do now! Since I've been here, I've seen things . . . horrible things . . . fetish-magic . . . and

all that sort of thing. I never believed
. . . But it *works* . . . '

He held up the mannikin between
thumb and finger.

'And who is this meant to represent?'

'Antoine Jacques, of course. Grey hair
. . . threads of clothes . . . no possibility of
a mistake there.'

'What do you want me to do about it?'
Seal asked

'I thought you might know of something we could do to — to stop it taking
effect. I don't understand how these
things work. If we just broke it up — I
don't know — we can't be certain what
effect it would have. It might be
dangerous! I braved a good deal to bring
it down to you, hoping to avert another
tragedy.'

'You think Miss Brown made this,
intending or hoping to do some harm to
Mr. Jacques by it?'

Prudence nodded, and drank some
iced water thirstily.

'You don't believe a word of any of this,
do you? But listen, do you remember the
day you found me standing on a chair

and I fainted into your arms? That was because I had unexpectedly found a sign of obeah, and as it was in my room I thought it was intended for me! I found out later that I was wrong. It had been placed there to plant suspicion on me should anything come to light about it later. What I found was a sheep's heart — buried in a flowerpot, and stuck through with long sharp needles. That was what made me faint.'

'I understand,' said Quentin sympathetically. 'Especially if you thought it was for you.'

'Yes. Well, I said and did nothing about it; but I watched it every day. And every few days there would be more needles piercing the heart. I was scared to death. Didn't know where it was all going to end. And then — and then the other day I found out what it meant and for whom it was intended. I overheard a conversation — or a quarrel, rather — between Miss Brown and her nephew. She was very, very angry with him. It seemed that he had created a terrible scene with Father Xavier and there had been no end of a hullabaloo, and Father Xavier had had a fearful heart attack and nearly died

'I think Raoul was a little frightened of Miss Brown, she was so very angry. He tried to excuse himself on the ground that he needed the money so desperately, was so hard-pressed that he would dare anything to get his hands on that great sum which he still felt rightfully belonged to him. Then she put on that horrible babyish whine of hers and said, didn't he trust his old aunt to get the money in the end? And if he needed ready cash in the meantime, why had he not asked her for it? Didn't they understand one another absolutely? Was it fair on her to go behind her back and try to squeeze the money out of the priest without telling her, without considering that such a move might wreck her plans? She knew what she was doing, she told him, and had things well under her control. Father Xavier's nerve was going. His servants were too scared to stay with him any more, on account of Julia's duppy which haunted the place ceaselessly . . .

'Raoul didn't like that at all. Evidently

he had not realised before exactly what her help involved. He guessed rather than understood the connection between the duppy's haunting and Miss Brown's interference, but it obviously made him uneasy. I could tell that he wanted to ask what she meant, and yet was afraid to put it into words. As for that hateful old woman, she rather enjoyed his discomfiture. She began to give him the lurid details, chuckling to herself all the while. Oh, it was disgusting!' Prudence shuddered and buried her face in her hands.

'She explained what she was doing to the priest and how she hoped thereby to attain her ends. She told Raoul about the heart buried in the flowerpot, and explained the ritual and significance of it. He was horrified, I'll say that much for him. 'It's taking effect,' she gloated. 'That last heart attack was really severe, and he's becoming quite ill and sick with pain now . . . ' I heard Raoul cry out in shocked tones: 'But it's no better than cruel, cold-blooded murder! How can you!' Then they started quarrelling again, hammer and tongs, but I didn't listen to any more. I sat there in a daze until I pulled myself together and got hold of the flowerpot. I threw it out of my window into the courtyard below, where it shivered to pieces. I stood there watching it, and wondering for the first time whether I'd done something very stupid and dangerous. Although I still refused to believe in superstitious nonsense, I prayed that my action would not harm the little priest in any way.

'Subconsciously, I noticed that it was quiet again; the quarrel was evidently over, but whether they had made it up again, I could not tell. As I stood at the window, I saw one of the cats come padding out of the front door and run sinuously to investigate the flowerpot. It sniffed and pawed about, and then gulped savagely at the heart. It swallowed it and then stood there uneasily, heaving and jerking and trying to throw it up again — in vain. It looked horrible. It was my fault, of course. But if I had called out I might have been discovered, and I dared not risk that.

'Just then Raoul came out, presumably

to go home — and seeing something was wrong, ran towards the cat and knelt down beside it among the debris. That was how Miss Brown found them . . . She immediately jumped to the conclusion that he was responsible for the tragedy. She snatched the frightened, contorted animal away from him and stalked with it into the house. Raoul followed behind, protesting uncomfortably his innocence.

'And then indoors it started all over again. And the cat died. And she swore she'd get even with him for it. And he — oh well, it went on and on, and then you came, and after a while it stopped . . . ' She smiled at him rather wanly. 'Now do you understand a little better?'

'Thank you for telling me. It makes a difference, of course. You never had time to tell Miss Brown you were responsible, but would you have done so if he had not been killed first?'

'You mean, you think Miss Brown killed him? That I am morally responsible for his death?' She shook her head. 'I don't agree,' she said firmly.

'I'm glad to know it wasn't merely a

sense of guilt that brought you to me. You came, then, because you really did hope that I could do something about this infernal mannikin. I'm afraid I can't think of anything sensible to do, barring going to her and telling her to stop it.' He looked at her. 'I guess that plan does not appeal to you?'

'I'm sure it would be dangerous. You don't know her as well as I do.'

'We might in that case try warning Jacques to be on his guard,' he suggested.

'That *would* be stupid! Once he is made to accept a suggestion like that, it gives the obeah twice as much power as before. I know that much. It is quite a usual thing for the victim to be warned of his doom by some sign or other, and his own belief in the black craft, and fear of it, makes him accept it as inevitable, and he submits to it. Don't forget that Jacques is a Creole and has lived here all his life. He must have often seen cases where it has worked. That knowledge would weaken his resistance fatally, believe me. No, there *must* be another way. And if there is, I shall find it. Don't bother about it anymore, Mr. Seal.' Tight-lipped, she began replacing the things in the pink bag.

'Wait, Miss Whitaker. I've had an idea. I know someone whom I believe has some experience of these things. He might be able to suggest something. Leave it with me and I'll show it to him the next time I see him.'

'I'd rather get it back in the place I took it from before she discovers its absence, if you don't mind. You can describe it to your friend when you meet him.'

'All right, I'll speak to Borodin about it — if I can find him — and then we'll see,' he promised.

'Borodin?' she said quietly. 'What do you know about Borodin?'

'*Not* the Russian composer, my dear. A very mere beachcomber I picked up, of the same name. Do you know him?'

'Why should you think that?'

'You are always so on the defensive, Miss Whitaker,' he complained. 'Now, don't look like that. Suppose you have got something to hide, why should you jump to the conclusion that I want to find out what it is? I don't imagine on that account that it has anything to do with this case. Stop imagining that I'm trying to ferret out your secret.'

She smiled reluctantly. 'I haven't anything of *that* sort on my mind.'

'Then tell me, why do you stay with Miss Brown if you're frightened of her?'

'It's my job, and it would be difficult to get another ... Nice of you to take an interest ... Are you any nearer finding out who murdered Raoul?'

'You know Mr. Foley has been arrested?'

'Oh, I'd forgotten. Do you think he did it?'

'Presumably so,' said Mr. Seal whimsically. 'Oh, don't put on your hat yet. Must you go already? But before you go, there is one little point that you could clear up for me.' He stared at her innocently. Leant forward persuasively. 'Now, who was in that boat — you know what I mean — on the night of the murder?'

'What makes you think I know?'

'You were so eager that Mr. Jacques should not see who it was. Almost panic-stricken, one might say.'

She stared before her thoughtfully, then said slowly, 'And if I said that it had nothing to do with the case, but was what you would call my private secret?'

'There is so much that requires to be explained in your story, Miss Whitaker, that I'm afraid I should not be satisfied to leave it at that.'

'I see.' Her tongue slid over her lips. 'Perhaps it would be better to explain, and trust that you will believe me this time and not carry it any further.

'It's awfully simple. The key — the one you thought strange I was able to identify — well, I'd been using it. Or, rather, I'd given it to a friend to use. He was a good, honest sort of chap, I believe, but absolutely on his beam-ends. He had nowhere to sleep. And I thought, those people up at the house, what would they care? They never use the place. Why shouldn't I let him sleep there? It would have been more sensible, I agree, to have asked permission, but you must have gathered by now what Miss Brown is like to me; I should never have heard the end of it. It was so much easier to slip the key off the ring and let him have it.

'He was very discreet. He slept there for a week or more and nothing went wrong. I used to go and see him sometimes. That was how I happened to go and look at the hut that night. I guessed something was wrong as soon as I saw the door open. But when I looked inside I nearly fainted with horror. My first thought — a stupid one — was that Raoul had come across my friend in there, they had had some kind of fight, and my friend had killed him. Naturally, I didn't want to get mixed up in it. Who would? You were quite right in your guess . . . I *was* running back to the house, leaving the corpse to be discovered by somebody else. Then I ran into you and pulled myself together pretty sharply. I felt awfully ashamed of myself. You know all the rest of that part.

'Then later,' she continued, 'I had a kind of premonition that he was in the boat. I don't know why. I know hardly anything about his life or how he keeps body and soul together. He certainly does not own a boat, but at that moment I could think of no one else who would want to land on that particular bit of shore. Obviously, I wanted him to get away unseen if it was humanly possible. I couldn't be certain that he had not been to the hut earlier that evening. And supposing, for an instant, that he had landed then and the key had been discovered on his person . . . He wouldn't have stood a dog's chance.' She sighed deeply.

'I would have told you all this before, but for one thing. I don't know what he was doing that night. A man in his position often has to do curious and unsavoury things for a livelihood. Suppose you were to accuse him of complicity in the crime and, rather than reveal the truth, he chose to remain silent? It might not be possible for him to produce an alibi. Do you understand?'

'Oh, yes, I think so. Really, you could speak to Borodin yourself about the spell-poppet, couldn't you? You evidently know him better than I do. It's quite obvious that your beachcomber is the same as mine. I'm very glad to know it. Besides,' he said caustically, but there was a twinkle in his eye, 'I shall be able to verify your story now.'

'So you will.'

'Forgive me not seeing you out, dear lady.'

He lay back on the lumpy pillows with a sigh of satisfaction as the door closed behind her.

12

The Root of All Evil

The day after Raoul's funeral — which was more subdued than La Morte's — Jacques was up in the long wooden offices bordering the west side of the cane plantations. Miss Brown seldom left the castle precincts, and Jacques had kindly offered to go up there and keep an eye on the business for her during his few free hours a day. It certainly was inconvenient having one's bailiff in jail, and she was grateful to Jacques for taking the responsibility off her shoulders. She was surprisingly ignorant of business affairs; they bored her to tears. She much preferred to pay someone to do her worrying for her.

The second day, when Jacques was beginning to find his way about among the numerous ledgers with their mysterious entries, Evelyn Foley came up. To lend a hand, she said. But it was more probable, Jacques thought, that it was to keep an eye on his activities. After all, it could hardly be taken for granted that a murderer was as innocent as a daisy in the field in all his other affairs. He was polite to her — he was naturally courteous — and it was scarcely the poor woman's fault that her husband was a murderer. She probably felt dreadful about it: she certainly looked it.

She looked drab and unattractive, sitting there in the sweltering heat hour after hour. Her white face looked flabby and unhealthy, like something that has lain sodden in water. She scarcely spoke, and when she did, addressed him curtly and briefly. She just sat there, watching him suspiciously but uncomprehendingly.

After a while he ignored her. He found plenty to absorb his interest. He wondered whether *she* knew anything.

Perhaps, if she did not know, she guessed. Perhaps that was why she went to Quentin finally, though she had sworn to herself that nothing would induce her to go. That is to say, technically, she didn't go to him — he came to her.

He noticed the difference in her at once: she showed her age now, though she made an effort to be as glamorous as ever when she came forward to greet him.

'It was nice of you to come,' she said, and her eyes filled with tears unexpectedly.

Mr. Seal, somewhat embarrassed, murmured: 'Not at all. Anything I can do to be of use.'

She patted her eyes with a fragment of cambric. 'You can have no idea how hateful everything has been lately. As for friends . . . I haven't seen a soul to speak to since — since it happened. That shows a nice thought on the part of one's so-called friends, doesn't it? But that isn't why I asked you to come, you may guess . . . Ulbear!' she called. And when he came, she said petulantly: 'There are no cigarettes, Ulbear.'

'No,' he said indifferently.

'But the box was nearly full. Where have they all gone?'

He spread out his hands insolently.

She bit her lip angrily and dismissed him.

'That is an example,' she told Quentin. 'Even the servants are rude to my face now. I suppose he stole the cigarettes. I don't mind that, though he'd never have dared to do it if Johnny were here. But the least he could have done was to buy some more out of the house-cash, and not leave me without one to bless myself with. And, on top of it, to be rude . . . Really, I don't know how I have the courage . . . '

He held out his case to her and she took one gratefully, leaning her slim fingers lightly against his hand as he tendered a match. Her thick black lashes cast a long shadow on her white cheek. He waited patiently. At last she burst out:

'Johnny didn't do it! It's not a bit of use you keeping him locked up there, you'll have to let him go in the end. He didn't do it . . . I suppose you've faked up some kind of a story out of that little trouble with Raoul. But it's all nonsense. As though Johnny *would* do it!'

'We have a little more to go on than that,' said Mr. Seal.

'Oh, the key!' she said scornfully. 'You may as well know right away that *I* put the key in his pocket. And he guessed it was me, I don't know why. So of course, being Johnny, he took all you said and allowed himself to be accused of murder and locked away, because he thought *I* must have done it, and he adores me. It was beastly of me not to have spoken before, but I was afraid — afraid of complicating matters, afraid of not being believed. Poor Johnny, married to a coward who lets him languish in a prison cell!'

'Won't you tell me how you came by the key and why you put it in poor Johnny's pocket, anyway?' said Mr. Seal persuasively.

'Funk, again. I couldn't think what to do with it. And I stuffed it into his pocket for a moment's respite while I tried to think what to do with the damned thing. It honestly wasn't because I wanted to throw the blame onto him, I swear by all that's sacred that it wasn't that. I just wanted to get it out of my sight for a bit. It was getting on my nerves. I put it in the

231

pocket of a suit he rarely wore, for one thing. But he found it. Whether it was some sort of telepathy . . . Or I wouldn't put it past that little sneak, Ulbear, to have discovered it — they know everything, those boys — and told him. However it was, Johnny must have got an awful fright, and done very much what I did. Locked it in his desk while he tried to figure what he had best do with it. But before he had time to think of anything, you hopped down on him and whisked him away.'

'I see. And how did it come into your possession?'

'I know you're going to be disagreeable. I had it because I was there. I mean, I took the key out of the hut door.'

Quentin frowned. '*Before* he was killed?'

'No. After. I was there all the time . . . I was actually there when he was killed!'

'What?' Quentin jumped. 'Then you *know* — '

'But I don't,' she cried. 'You've *got* to believe me. I don't know anything. Not who or how.'

'Suppose you explain exactly what *did* happen,' Seal said gently.

She burst into tears and began to wring her hands.

'Oh, my God, how shameful it is! I hardly know how to tell you . . . I told you how he begged me to see him again. Of course, I knew he loved me, and I used to tease him about it, but I felt sorry for him too and I didn't think it would do any harm to go. That was my mistake. I'd never been really alone with him before. I saw at once that he was in a state of feverish excitement. He seized me in his arms and began to kiss me furiously. He was so wildly passionate that I began to feel afraid. After a minute, I pushed him away. At least, I tried to. He wouldn't listen. He pushed me towards the bunk, and almost before I knew it he had thrust me onto it. I was alone with him in that squalid little hut, nowhere near anywhere. It was beastly!' She put her hands over her face. 'Even if I had not been too ashamed, it would have been useless to call. No one would have heard. He was awfully strong. Panic and darkness mounted into my head. I was afraid I was going to faint. I could feel my resistance weakening. And then — '

She dropped her hands into her lap again, and lifted her head to stare at Quentin unseeingly. 'And then he gave a kind of grunt or groan, and sort of slumped down against me with all his weight. He didn't move again ... I couldn't think what had happened. I spoke to him, and when he didn't answer, I imagined that he'd been taken ill — had some sort of a fit, perhaps. I tried to sit up, to push him away. I put my arm round him to sort of lift him, do you see, and — ' She made a hideous grimace. ' — and I felt something sticking horribly out of his back ... and round about it was all wet and sticky ... How I didn't faint or go mad or die, I don't know. If you can imagine it, lying there in the hot darkness with a dead thing on top of you!' She gave a little moan of horror and shivered. 'If only it hadn't been dark. That was what made it so utterly horrible. I couldn't get out of there fast enough. With all my strength I pushed him up and slid from underneath his body. The pillow fell to the ground, but I didn't dare to pick it up in case there was blood on my fingers. I let him fall back in the position he had been in before. I scrambled over to the door, nearly frantic. He had locked it behind me as I came in. There was no handle, you know. I unlocked it and opened the door with the key, but I didn't dare leave it behind me. I took it with me and fled. I don't think it was till I got home that I really grasped the fact that he had been murdered . . . cold-bloodedly murdered. What could I do then? It was too late. It terrified me even more than before. I almost wished I had left the key behind. I couldn't think how to get rid of it. In the end, I just shoved it into Johnny's pocket, as I told you.

'Now that I've explained it to you, you'll let Johnny go, won't you . . . ?' Her voice died away and she waited for him to speak.

'It doesn't rest with me, Mrs. Foley. I'll tell them what you have told me, and of course that does alter the situation, but — '

She stood up quickly. 'Why shouldn't they let him go? He never had the key at all, don't you see?'

'Yes,' he said patiently, 'I know he never had the key; but you see, he didn't need it in order to murder Raoul, did he? You showed me that yourself, Mrs. Foley. Whoever it was who killed Raoul never came into the hut at all. For one thing, the door was locked and the key in the lock. For another, you neither saw nor heard anyone.'

Her lower jaw began to tremble, and she drew back.

'You're not suggesting that I — '

'I have only suggested that no third person opened that door — that no third person entered the hut ... unless, of course, you would like me to believe that the murderer was already established in the hut before you arrived, and did not leave until after you had fled. But in that case, he must also have been established before Raoul came; and if so, why did he not kill Raoul at once? Why wait until you appeared, creating unnecessary complications? Though of course,' he added thoughtfully, 'you may have been an integral part of his scheme. There's that to be considered. For instance, if Foley were genuinely suspicious and jealous, he might, having found out about this proposed meeting, have gone down there on purpose to have his worst fears confirmed.'

'You devil!' she cried, pushing her hands at him furiously. 'You know very well it isn't true. It didn't happen like that at all. As though I shouldn't have known if there was anyone else in the hut. It's hardly big enough to swing a cat in. Do you think I wouldn't have heard his breathing? Do you think he would have stood there and allowed me to be assaulted under his very nose? Are you mad?'

Mr. Seal picked up his panama and sauntered to the door pensively.

'I don't see that it's any more unlikely on the face of it than for you to stand there and wait for Raoul to take his pants and shoes off before 'assaulting' you. Good morning, Mrs. Foley.'

★ ★ ★

Arriving back at the Royal Splendide, he was told that there was someone to see him. In the stuffy parlour with its bead curtains, its coconut matting and dusty antimacassars, the priest's small black form rose up to greet him.

'I hope you have not been waiting long, Father?'

'Not at all. If you are busy, I shall go away and return at some more convenient time.' It almost seemed as though he wanted to go, but Quentin persuaded him to stay.

'Do you want to speak to me privately, Father?'

'Yes, there is something. I think perhaps you will be able to help me.' He licked his lips. 'Could we — perhaps a little walk, do you think?'

Quentin concurred amiably with the suggestion, anxious to learn what the priest had to say.

They soon escaped Wigtown and walked inland to the swampy glades. Trees and ferns and creepers grew together in a luxuriant screen, whose dripping green fronds obscured the sun.

The colouring was wonderfully rich, marred by the overpowering smell of rotting vegetation. A family of black pigs went squealing and stumbling across their path. They might have been in the heart of the jungle a million miles from anywhere. Quentin wondered whether the priest had any reason for taking him this way. Whether he intended some mischief? Really, he was developing a mind like a cheap thriller! Still, he was secretly glad to see a tall black woman in a sugar-pink Mother Hubbard dress come swinging down the path towards them with an immense pile of clean laundry balancing on her head, and to know the parts were not as uninhabited as they seemed.

''*Jour, Mon Père*,' she sang.

''*Jour, ma fille*.' And when she had passed out of earshot, he turned to Quentin and said simply: 'It's the money. It's bothering my conscience. You see, I tried to put it from me for a long time by pretending that it was nothing to do with me really, that the money was only mine in trust, that it really belonged to the Church. The end justified the means, that's what I tried to think.' He pushed his hat farther back on his head. 'But now, I feel like a kind of Judas. I don't know how to act. I thought perhaps you would be so good as to advise or help me.' He raised round brown eyes to Mr. Seal's appealingly.

'I'd like to understand a little more about it first.'

'Well, if it had not been for that ignorant atheist of a doctor, I might never have known anything about it. He believes, you see, that Madame Jacques died of a secondary stroke or something, and that she was dead before the cat jumped on her.

'He apparently did not discover anything in the post-mortem to show when or how she died. But he reasons that if the cat killed her, it would be only natural to expect to find that she had inhaled some cat's hairs either through the nose or mouth. Or there would be fur in her teeth, I think. Well, he found nothing! So he at once assumed that it was because she was already dead. I suppose it's logical enough. Only I happen to have other information.

'Mind you, I'm still not sure, only it seems too much of a coincidence otherwise. And of course, if I *am* right in my suspicions, then ought I to accept, in God's name, what is neither more nor less than tainted money? That's my problem, Mr. Seal.'

'I'm sorry, but I still don't understand just what the problem is. Why do you think the money is tainted? And why aren't you satisfied with the doctor's report, even though he is an atheist?'

'I believe the poor creature committed suicide. Yes, truly. Bear in mind that I knew her, in her latter years, perhaps better than anyone else. It was to me that she revealed her secret thoughts and fears. And do you suppose the poor soul was happy, or even contented? I did what I could, but put yourself in her place and imagine what you would feel. If there had been any *hope* . . . but there wasn't, and she knew it; knew also that her life might stretch on, burdensome and boring, for years and years. She always felt herself to be a drag on her family. In fact, her mental state was worse than her physical one. I am convinced that she would have killed herself long since if she had ever had the means. But you can see how impossible it was for her — watched day and night, so to speak, and absolutely helpless; even if means of some sort had been left near her, she would not have been able to use them. I sympathised, though I did my best to show her how wrong and wicked it was to think like that. But evidently my best was not good enough.' He looked almost ready to cry.

Mr. Seal could understand all that. But since it was impossible, considering the nature of her malady, for her to kill herself, what made him think that she had somehow contrived to after all?

'That sister of hers,' mumbled the priest bitterly. 'She had got that poor child interested in her trickery and mumbo-jumbo. I'm not saying that she was deliberately planning mischief, mind you. Perhaps she genuinely thought it would benefit and distract Madame Jacques. Why, on that very last day when I went to visit her, I found Miss Brown with her, reading to her from a book on mesmerism, and they told me quite openly that they had been trying it and had made several successful experiments. Of course, I can't vouch for the truth of that, but her sister, I could see, was as enthusiastic as her unhappiness permitted her to show. I reproach myself now that I did not do more to dissuade her from the practice. Then, when the cat came into the room, you remember, she wanted me to leave it there, she tried to convey that she had willed it to come up to her. A notion that I naturally pooh-poohed. But supposing I was mistaken, Mr. Seal? Supposing that after I left, when she found herself quite alone and undisturbed, she did somehow or other will the animal to come into her room, to jump on to her bed, to do just what everyone was so careful that it should not do — smother her? If she went as far as that, it is only to be expected that she would hold her breath and die without struggling, and that would be why no hair was found in her nose and mouth. She practically willed herself to die.'

'I suppose it is possible,' said Mr. Seal. 'If one is desperate enough one will do anything. But what a singularly uncomfortable way to die! You never mentioned this possibility to the doctor?'

Father Xavier looked a little ashamed.

'I thought it wiser not to say anything . . . until I had made up my mind what to do, at any rate.'

'And now you have?'

'I'm afraid so,' he sighed. 'I shall have to give up the money.'

'Isn't it a little late for that now? Raoul is already dead.'

The priest frowned. 'You're not trying to tell me that the one has anything to do with the other? Was it because of the money that he was killed?'

'It may have been the indirect cause,' said Quentin cautiously. 'There was a lot of trouble about it, wasn't there? All on his side, I agree. But he behaved very unpleasantly to you, didn't he?'

'If *I* had been killed, now,' suggested the priest, with a three-cornered smile, 'it would be more understandable, wouldn't it?'

'Well, it would not have been very easy for Raoul to prove his innocence. He threatened so openly to kill you, you know. But still, we're getting away from the subject. It is a great pity, if you have definitely made up your mind that you are not entitled to the money, that you did not come out with it a few days ago and obviate all this tragedy.'

'So you do think I ought to return the money.'

'I never said so. I certainly shouldn't do anything in a hurry. You still have nothing to go on beyond surmise. You may be quite wrong.'

'I know,' the priest said, impatiently. 'That's why it has taken me so long to make up my mind. If I am right, then it is blood-money, and should not be used for holy things. Though I can't see how the truth can ever be known in this case. But if the money is tainted, then my ignorant assumption that La Morte died a natural death, shall we say, does not alter that basic fact, and I am acting on my own mistaken judgment instead of the reality. Therefore, I have come to the conclusion that it might be best to be on the safe side and reject the money.'

'There's surely no hurry to decide one way or the other. Raoul, who was the chief person interested in the money, is dead. It is possible that when this case has cleared up a bit more we *shall* know whether La Morte died of natural causes or not. I shouldn't say anything definite till then, if I were you. If I find out anything useful I will let you know.'

As Quentin walked back to Wigtown he could not but think it odd that Hattie and her mumbo-jumbo had come into the picture again. Did all these people believe in it, or did they not? Was there anything to believe in? Was it to frighten them into obedience to her whims, or did she believe it herself? To what limits could hypnotism carry you?

13

The Zombie Walks

The priest's conversation left Quentin feeling worried and restless. Eventually, he yielded to his conscience, and climbed up early next morning to inspect La Morte's room in the upper storey. It had been left as it was, except for a large paisley shawl draped across the bed in graceful disguise.

He discreetly opened the drawers, inspected the letters lying in the bureau, surveyed the unworn dresses hanging in the cupboard. Anything of importance there had been removed. He noticed this time the netting over the ledge beneath the window, presumably to prevent the animals clambering up and entering that way. So the cat *must* have come in through the open door. Was it the same cat that Prudence had killed accidentally with the sheep's heart? That would be poetic justice. Probably it was, and that was why Hattie had jumped to the conclusion that Raoul had deliberately killed it out of revenge. But then that implied that Hattie knew she was to blame . . .

He sat down and stared blankly at the little white-painted wooden table before him. A big bottle of surgical spirit on one side, and a great jar of cotton wool on the other . . . little bottles of coloured liquids, inscribed with mysterious Latin abbreviations . . . a box of thin-necked glass phials, rubber-sealed . . . blunt-ended scissors . . . a pair of tweezers . . . a hypodermic in a neat nickel-plated case . . . a medicine glass . . .

But Quentin was reviving his memory of that fatal afternoon. First, Hattie had been reading to her sister a treatise on the human will. And then the priest had come in, as he was expected to, seen what they were reading, and possibly voiced his disapproval. Then Hattie had left, and Julia was alone with her father confessor. They had talked — according to the priest — of mesmerism and death, and presumably of other things too. Then, as he left, the cat came in, and after a little parley was ejected again. The nurse took over from Father Xavier. It was her day out, and likely enough her one interest was to get away without loss of time. She tidied her patient, waiting for Prudence to relieve her. She gave her the injection. And then there was no more to be done. Quentin automatically counted the ampoules: there were twelve little cotton nests, and only seven of them still filled. Above each nest was written the date on which it had been used. No mistake there. However, they were large ampoules, big enough to hold two cubic centimetres; perhaps the entire contents were not used in one injection. But, though he was unfamiliar with that particular prescription, he could tell by the listed contents on the label of the box that it was a harmless enough sedative, and that even if she had been injected with all twelve phials at once she would not have been very much the worse for it, at least not to the point of death. So it wasn't *that*. To continue, then . . .

The nurse had waited no longer for Prudence, confident that she would not fail her. But Prudence, on a rather insincere story, *had* failed her, nor had the sense to go up and explain; instead, she'd trusted to Raoul to stay until she returned. She had promised to be gone not more than five minutes or so; but even if that was just a manner of speaking, there was a wide gulf between that and the three hours she actually took. In three hours, anything might have happened to Julia, and so it had.

Still, Raoul had come up and stayed with his mother for a while. Presumably she had been all right then. Or was she? He was, so far as was known, the last person to see her alive. He had taken the opportunity to remove her purse and money. He could have just as easily said she had given it to him when its loss was discovered. Had he not thought of that? Yet, if she had been alive, he would not have been able to say it — so perhaps he had already thought out his story and, even after he found the situation changed, had decided it would be best to stick to it.

Then, presuming that she was alive when he left the room — leaving also the door open behind him — she somehow died between that moment and Quentin finding her. He himself had met Raoul racing headlong down the steps just before he started up them. Allowing all due time for rests and meditation on the way, it could surely not have been more than twenty minutes before he peered in at that window and saw her. Twenty minutes for her to die. And how long would it take to smother someone? Much less. And the servants were all away, too. And Hattie lay downstairs asleep.

Suddenly he struck his forehead with his knuckles.

'Bonehead!' he exclaimed. 'You've been misleading yourself, you fool. It didn't need anyone to do it; it was already done. Good God, is it possible? Then, even if anything went wrong, no one would know . . . A chance in a million . . . But how in heaven's name am I going to prove it? Supposing I am mistaken?'

On the way down he stepped in to see Miss Brown and tell her that her bailiff

251

was likely to be released that day.

'I don't know why you think that interests me,' she said, sweeping Orlando off the only chair that was not loaded up and into her arms, 'though it was good of you to come and tell me. But now you are here, do sit down and amuse me. You're not looking for a job, by any chance? No, I thought not. But it really is sickening about that wretch Foley. Antoine says he's been robbing me for years, and I never should have known had it not been for this. And how is one to get anyone trustworthy out here? Naturally, I knew that Foley was making his job as soft as possible. And took it for granted that he was out here as a matter of personal convenience. No one who was not obliged to would come and live out here in this Godforsaken spot . . . However, it just happens to suit me. It's lackadaisical and free, and I'm used to it, having lived here nearly all my life. But for a man with ambitions, what does it offer?'

'Quite a lot, evidently, if one augments one's income with judicious thieving,' laughed Quentin.

'Well, yes, there is that. And what I'm to do now, I don't know. I almost wish that Uncle Antoine hadn't told me. Where ignorance is bliss . . . eh? Still, Jacques says it runs into thousands of francs.'

'But if you've suspected him all these years and been content to let sleeping dogs lie, why should you mind now?'

'I can't pretend ignorance now, can I? That would be condoning crime,' she said sanctimoniously.

'Why not just give him a good talking-to when he comes out, and offer to take him back if he promises not to do it again? He'd be so relieved that you were not going to prosecute him that he'd swear anything. And into the bargain you've got something to keep him up to the mark with.'

'A murderer! No, thanks.'

'Murderer? But he's being released.'

'He's being released, therefore he can't be guilty, says he!' she exclaimed derisively. 'I thought you were supposed to be doing a little detective work, yourself over this business . . . I must say, I don't think much of your conclusions.'

'I'm inclined to agree with you. Would it be indelicate in the circumstances to inquire your reasons for regarding your ex-bailiff as Raoul's murderer?'

'Orlando, I don't think we'd better say anything. We'd better leave it all to dawn on Mr. Seal the super-sleuth by degrees . . . Of course, I'm only pulling your leg! But I don't think it would look very well to take him on again until the — er — real murderer has been found. Besides, I don't believe Jacques would ever forgive me. He was terribly indignant over his discovery about Foley. Had he not already been in jail, I think he would have skinned him alive. And when they let him out again, I don't know how I am to avoid prosecuting him without annoying Jacques. He's been so kind, I hate to seem ungrateful.' She sighed.

'If Jacques wants me to prosecute, I will. It's the least I can do to show my gratitude for his going through all those hateful ledgers! He's rather fond of me, I suppose. Or do you imagine that only my animals could be fond of an ugly old image like me?'

He hastily repudiated the idea, murmuring indistinctly of charm.

'It's wretched for a woman on her own. She's nothing but prey for men like Foley. Of course, Antoine said if he had only *realised*, he would have looked into it long ago. But with Julia on his mind, and one thing and another . . . Life hasn't been easy for him either, I dare say.'

'It was beastly for him, losing his wife like that.'

'Oh, beastly,' she agreed absently. She bent over the gibbon and tossed it ecstatically squealing into the air. 'Oh, wicked, wicked one, what a lot you know behind that velvet mask, and what a lot you can never tell!' she laughed. 'Have you ever waited for anything a long time, Mr. Seal, so long that your heart almost failed and you thought you would never attain your desire? At last, after nearly twenty-five years — a lifetime, Mr. Seal — I see the first faint glimmerings that my dream is coming true. It's almost unbelievable!' Her eyes sparkled like aquamarines and her whole face shone. She laughed and clapped her hands on her thighs.

'That must be very gratifying indeed,' he said gravely.

'My God, I'll say it's gratifying! It's worth everything to me.' And her smile became a savage and feline grin. 'Oh, yes, it'll be worth everything.'

'They say that when one has achieved one's goal, everything seems not more pleasurable, but unprofitable and stale. You aren't afraid of that, evidently?'

Her whole body quivered with silent mirth.

'My God, I'm not. Lead me to the altar, Charlie, and I'll do the rest.'

'And will it be soon now?'

'Ah-ha, naughty boy, wouldn't you like to know!' She poked a finger into his chest.

'In any case, I hope you will allow me to wish you much happiness.'

The conversation became impersonal, and after a while Quentin was able to make his escape. He went down the steps rapidly.

He was commencing to experience a little fear. He could just perceive that events were rolling up like great thunder-clouds to some hidden climax at which he could only guess. It was up to him to step in first. But he knew that it would be useless to attempt to step in unless he was ready and really understood what he was doing. He would have to hurry. He would need to see Borodin and the doctor, too, and if necessary he would have to kidnap Napoleon.

Suddenly, he began to laugh. He had a vision of Evelyn Foley's expression when she learnt that her husband had lost his job, and all her fairy tales had been of no use at all. Would she kick up one hell of a shindy or be very quiet and pathetic? Funny that the two women who had been most interested in the dead boy should now clash once again. Jealousy! The same old theme.

Fortunately, the doctor was in and could see him. He sat down in the cool consulting-room and tried to marshal his thoughts. It was beginning to get hot already, and he mopped his face, aware of the doctor's sharply professional eye watching him,

'It's not about myself. It's about La Morte, Madame Jacques, you know. I'm going to ask you to do something rather unusual, doctor. I want you to examine the corpse again.'

The doctor bounced forward in his chair.

'But that is not possible!'

'It sounds unreasonable, but it must be done. You see, I have discovered some fresh facts about her death. I don't believe it was as we thought at all. I believe that if we exhumed her, we should find — '

'There has been a P.M. already, my dear sir, and there was nothing.'

'That was because you didn't know what to look for. This time I shall be able to tell you.'

'You would have to be very sure of your facts indeed before you could get an order to exhume the body. In fact, I don't believe you could get one at all.'

'That is exactly the point. And even if we could get a permit, we don't want to arouse a lot of suspicion and nastiness in people's minds, do we? Much better to be discreet, don't you think?'

'I do,' said the doctor emphatically. 'I think people who stir up mud have nothing but themselves to thank if they get into trouble.'

'I'm afraid you have no social conscience. One cannot let murderers roam around loose, you know.'

'Murder?' repeated the other in surprise. 'I dare say that will be a plea of insanity or justifiable homicide — '

'Justifiable nuts!' said Mr. Seal rudely. 'You think it's going a little far? I want to prevent it going a damn sight further. I'm not making it up. But being satisfied myself isn't enough; I've got to have proof, and I've got to have it soon. All I ask of you is to make the examination and analysis. *And to say nothing about it.* Surely you can do that without involving yourself too much in what you seem to feel is not your concern anymore.'

The doctor smiled. 'I daresay I could manage that without undue scruples. But how am I to apply for an exhumation grant? On what grounds?'

'Suppose you leave that to me, sir. If I see to that and convey the body to you, will you do the rest?'

The doctor hedged inquisitively. Mr. Seal leant forward and whispered. If one knew nothing, one could not answer awkward questions. The doctor nodded.

So he went back to the Royal Splendide for a siesta during the fierce noonday heat, while he pondered on a plan of campaign. Borodin would contrive something. Borodin, thank the Lord, was venal and unscrupulous.

As soon as the sun had moved slightly from the perpendicular, he went in search of the beachcomber. He found him lying beneath the stripy shade of a palm-tree, his hat over his face.

'I have a little job for you, my friend,' said Quentin insidiously.

Boris removed his hat lazily.

'Have you ever heard of a spell-poppet?' Quentin began, dropping down beside him. He described the one Prudence had shown him, and Borodin nodded wisely and explained the purpose and usage of the fetish — which was not identical with Prudence's version.

Quentin rubbed his hands gleefully. 'Exactly so. And now for the job. A little theft — or not even that, it's only borrowing for a few hours . . . Not difficult for you, but important, very important . . . It's a matter of life and death. Now. Listen — '

And he propounded to the Russian exactly how the unpleasant task ahead of them could be achieved with the minimum danger and discomfort.

But Boris, once he understood what Quentin was talking about, proved unexpectedly obstinate.

'But why?' wailed Quentin irritably. 'You're an adventurer, aren't you? You're going to be well paid. What are you kicking at? Don't you consider that I'm offering enough money in proportion to the risk you run? Then tell me your price and I'll see if I can meet it.'

'It is not a question of the money,' groaned the Russian. 'I have no papers, I am done for. They are all lost, stolen, and without them I can do nothing. My *identity* papers! At any moment the police may demand to see them. And if they found me doing anything so terrible as you suggest, it would be all up with me.'

'Oh, you needn't worry about that! The head constable here is a friend of mine. I'll make it all right with him,' said Quentin casually.

'My God, sir, if you betray me I will kill you,' he threatened vehemently, twixt fear and fury.

Mr. Seal maintained an ambiguous silence.

'Whatever happens, do not mention such a thing to the police! Do not mention it to anyone! I told you in confidence, simply to explain why I was not able to oblige you in this little matter.'

'Of course, if you help me I shall not mention it to anyone. Why should I? But if you do not help me . . . I might find it necessary to inform the police, if only in order to distract their attention from my own performances. Do you understand me?'

Borodin glared. 'You would become a pigeon's stool?' he said contemptuously.

'A stool-pigeon,' corrected Mr. Seal.

He was discovering a hidden charm in blackmail, a delightful sense of power. He naturally had no intention of telling the police — or anyone — about Borodin's sad case. And, as Seal later pointed out to him, if he undertook the job and was well paid for it, he would at least have a little something with which to bribe the incorruptible representatives of the law, and so would be that much better off. An argument with which Boris could not but agree. So it was settled.

★   ★   ★

Black shadows were grouping by the trees at the edge of the plantation. The moon had not yet risen. From the shadows issued a faint, monotonous humming, swelling to a chant. Muffled drumbeats took it up, thudding like a frightened heart. Two of the shadows detached themselves from the rest and beat round rhythmically in a circle. One after another joined in, till there was one stamping, frenzied, circular movement. Gradually it subsided again. Shadows crept back to the watchful trees. Only one remained in the centre of the circle, erect and motionless as a column, dimly outlined against the deep sapphire sky in a waiting posture, head flung backwards, breasts tilting sharply up.

Silence, but for the thudding of a frightened heart. Suddenly a cock's strident crowing shattered the eerie quiet, a crowing that was cut off sharply in mid-cry as if by Death's sickle. Silence again for the space of a breath. And then the crowing recommenced, with a long-drawn shivering screech, that issued from the now-animated quivering figure standing in the centre of the circle, in a ghostly inhuman crow. Then it died away, and the shadows swept forward once more.

Down in Wigtown, within the precincts of the police station, Mr. Seal leant forward confidentially to Brigadier Orage and spoke in low tones. The brigadier listened attentively.

Mr. Seal was passing on information he had received (no, he could not say how or from whom) that there was to be a session of Island voodoo that very night.

Naturally he had brought the news to his friend without hesitation. Of course, there might really be nothing in it, but it would be worth while investigating the affair on the off-chance. It would always be useful to know just who participated in these affairs, however unimportant they were. If that much was discovered, it would not have been a vain expedition. But the whole thing *might* be important. And even if it should prove too big a thing for him to handle on his own, there was still no harm done, and the police would be that much wiser. Yet, though Napoleon saw the wisdom of Mr. Seal's remarks, he was strangely reluctant to interfere. He stoutly denied that this was because he was afraid of that native nonsense. Perhaps it alarmed him to think that anyone significant might be there. Of course, under Seal's combined gentle ridicule and firm insistence, he caved in eventually. Mr. Seal politely declined to accompany him. That might be thought a little odd, but Mr. Seal had other fish to fry.

It was on the way there, actually

between the church and the plantations, that Napoleon saw it advancing on him with a slow mechanical shuffle, eyes bent unseeingly on the ground, arms hanging along the body. Its long pale hair gleamed faintly as it fell limply over its shoulders in the still air. He had not the least doubt in the world who it was. Though he doubted his own identity, he doubted everything *but* that. His heart was paralysed in his throat, stopping his breath. He could feel the blood ebbing away from his fingers and toes. For a measureless moment he endured that steady advance, and then he wrenched his rooted legs out of the path and fled . . .

The shadows scattered and melted at his approach. He tried to scream a warning. 'A zombie!' he cried, in a voice no bigger than a breath, and fell on his knees in the centre of the circle, and toppled over on his side . . .

Not, he knew, that a zombie had any power to harm him. A zombie was no more than a magically-animated corpse, subservient as a robot to the master-magician who had called it up. As a rule they were utilised for work, labour that was not only cheap but free. Solitary, peculiar old women were often reputed to have bands of them working for them in the fields from dusk to dawn, willy-nilly, instead of hiring living workers by day. Soulless, will-less, mindless; toiling silently through the dark until another dawn permitted them to slip back wearily into their vacant graves. Gruesome, pathetic labourers.

No, it was not of the zombie that Napoleon was so scared, but of having recognised it for who it was. For it was none other than La Morte shuffling so relentlessly along the narrow track, she who had not walked or moved for so long, she who had not lain more still in her grave than she had lain in her bed. It was enough to frighten a braver man than Napoleon.

The first person he wanted to know about it was Quentin; he had to find him at all costs. But when finally he ran across him, Quentin laughed. He tried to disguise it, but he laughed nevertheless, and pooh-poohed the idea as moonshine.

Napoleon was hurt by his European agnosticism. The upshot of it was that one of them suggested they go over to the cemetery for a look-see.

Tall trees swayed above the open grave with its upturned earth and scattered clods. The zinc-lined coffin was empty.

'There!' gasped Napoleon triumphantly.

'It may be as you say,' Mr. Seal admitted, with a show of reluctance, and modestly shuffled an obliterating shoe-sole over an all-too-human footprint.

The funniest thing of all — though to Napoleon it was the last obvious proof — was that the next morning all was as it had been before, the earth above the grave pressed down just as though it had never been touched.

So Napoleon was satisfied.

And Mr. Seal was satisfied too. The doctor had found that his supposition was correct. That which should have been present in the cadaver was not there.

And Borodin had a comforting little rustle of notes next to his skin, so he too was not displeased with life. He was optimistic about the future. Perhaps he was going to be able to recoup himself after all for his losses on that disastrous night when he had dropped his papers in the sea and lost so much else besides. If he could make good, sooner or later Prudence would forgive him. If his next coup was successful, he would be able to buy new papers, faked or real ... and then ...

14

San Rocca

The Feast of San Rocca, the patron saint of the Island, was quite an important affair at which all colours and creeds were represented. All the shops were shut for the day; it was an Island holiday.

There was a procession with banners that sauntered all around over Wigtown. And dancing in the Square. But it was not till nightfall that it really got going.

From Jacques' house, one could see the many-coloured dragon snaking through the narrow streets, the banners jutting out on its neck like a bright mane.

Hattie watched it inattentively. She looked ill. Her eyes were sunken and seemed colourless and dull. Her stubby fingers picked nervously at her dress. She admitted she had not slept well. Her brother-in-law was so sympathetic; was she worrying about anything? He wanted to know.

When she spoke, her voice had lost its usual malice, her tone uncertain. It was a thing she felt chary of mentioning, and yet . . . He had, she supposed, heard about the zombie and Julia's empty grave?

Oh yes, he had. But surely she was not taking that kind of native nonsense seriously, was she?

Hattie squeezed Jacques' arm convulsively.

'Don't laugh at me, darling. I don't like it. After all, I have studied these things, Antoine. And I'm sure there's something fishy about this. It alarms me. If it never happened, why should they say it did? That policeman can't be altogether stupid. And anyway, it doesn't depend on his testimony alone: Mr. Seal saw the empty grave himself. If you still think it isn't true, why do you suppose *he* is pretending it is?'

'But, my dear, aren't you seeing this a little out of proportion? It's been a series of shocks and a prolonged strain for you. Some people bear up wonderfully at the time and only feel the full shock of it weeks later. That's what has happened in your case. You've done so much for all of us — so much for me in particular,' he said gratefully, 'and now you're paying the price.'

'It's sweet of you, Antoine, but it isn't that.'

'Of course it is. Look here, when there was all that business with the priest, when he was supposed to be haunted by Julia's duppy night after night, you didn't bother your head about it. And yet now you're feeling all upset about it. It isn't reasonable, my dear.'

'That was different. That was obviously rot. But this is serious, Antoine: it's interfering with the peace of the dead. Something sacred. I'm surprised you don't feel that yourself.'

'My dear, I simply don't believe in it. So far as I am concerned, Julia's gone, she's no longer in that body at all. And I don't believe she'd care a bit what was done to her body, even if she knew about it.'

She looked at him strangely. 'You miss

the point. Why should anyone want Julia's lifeless body?'

'I never thought of that,' he admitted slowly. 'And that was what kept you awake all night?'

'I couldn't help feeling perturbed about it,' she assented.

He looked somewhat perturbed himself. He was wondering how it could have kept her awake worrying all night, when it had not taken place until the middle of the night, and it certainly should not have come to her ears (as it had not to his) until the morning. He worried at her knowing about it. And this Mr. Seal, where did he come into it? Had he made a mistake, after all, in soliciting his amateur help on the case?

The procession came sauntering down Cariba Walk, passing the Royal Splendide; colourful, with suits of royal blue and mauve and light tan, cut in perilously at the waist and with overbalancing shoulders and lapels, brightly-striped shirts and jaunty fluttering ties. The shoes were either yellow or pointed patent-leather. Hair had been flattened with fixative to a shiny slab. As for the girls, their customary bandanas and patchwork of gay colours were gone. They teetered along in their high-heeled shoes, their legs showing darkly through the pink cotton or rayon stockings, contrasting oddly with their bare brown arms. The dresses were mostly muslin or voile in pastel colours. And, perched atop their cropped heads, they wore hats of crinoline straw on which nestled posies and roses and splendid feathers, rather crushed now. Some of the more intensely refined even wore white cotton gloves.

They were accompanied by the metallic wheeze of accordions and the rhythmic beat of drums, in a repetitive melody of a few bars. There seemed to be an endless number of verses, the words of which were unintelligible to Quentin, but which he guessed, from the laughter and rolling eyes with which each set was greeted, to be ribald. The chorus he made out to be simply:

San Roc-ca,
Hey! Hey!

San Roc-ca,
Hey! Hey!

A run of three notes up and then a fourth down, twice, abruptly accented on the drums, and then the five notes reversed. It caught at your brain maddeningly.

Napoleon leant against the wooden posts of the veranda and looked at Quentin.

'How are you liking it?'

'They certainly seem to be enjoying themselves. How long does it last?'

'Reckon it'll go on till morning. When they get tired, they just lie down. They can still have as much fun lying down!' He grinned superbly.

A pretty yellow-skinned girl with a hat pulled saucily over one eye came dancing up, jiggling breasts thrusting invitingly against her thin, sweat-damp blouse. A slender arm went round the policeman's neck.

'*Toi, beau garçon,*' she remarked.

'Git along, gal,' he said calmly. 'You and me is milk and lemon.' He removed the arm and turned his back on her. It was plain that he felt the grandeur and responsibility of his position very keenly.

'You were telling me about San Rocca,' Quentin said. 'Who was he?'

'He's no good; a low, good-for-nothing saint if ever there was one.'

'That's new on me. I never heard of having a patron saint who was a ne'er-do-well. How did he ever make the grade, then?'

'They say San Rocca was such a damn bad lot when alive that he make everybody else seem quite bang full of virtue. He took all the sins on his shoulders, he said, so everybody else could go free.'

'Big of him! Better than hiding away in a cave and only saving your own soul.'

'Yeah! But San Rocca had all the fun too. He had all the sweet times, the gals and drink . . . But pretty soon they are going to take him out to sea and drown him dead. No more San Rocca. No more trouble till next year.'

'That's a grand idea. A pity more of us haven't thought of that way out. Have a fine big party and chuck all your troubles into the sea before you even get them. So everyone's happy on Apostle Island and nothing ever goes wrong, eh?'

'I guess you know better than that, sir. Old Rocca, he does not stay dead. After fun comes troubles, as night comes after day. Plenty of trouble tomorrow, you bet,' he promised.

The death and burial of San Rocca was the high spot of the festival. That part of the ceremony only took place after dark. It was for this spectacle that everybody assembled.

Crowds drifted down to Wigtown harbour. The harbour and the Bay beyond were starred irregularly with little clusters of coloured lights hanging from the rigging of the shadowy boats. And low in the sky hung a ruddy-gold moon. It was very hot . . . Quentin wiped his face. Gusts of warm cloying air blew from inland, gently rocking the little boats. Anyone who owned a craft was in a favourable position that night. Music and laughter eddied across the water.

He heard someone below hail him by

name. He leant over the side of the jetty, and there was Prudence, laughing up at him from a little cockleshell of a boat with an outboard motor. It was attached by a painter to one of the slimy posts of the jetty, against which it bumped gently to and fro.

'Halloo there!' she cried. 'Come on down, why don't you?'

He scrambled over and landed with a thud.

'It was nice of you to call me.'

'We're both friendless and far from home. I thought we'd enjoy it more together.'

'Oh well, I'm off-duty and out to enjoy myself tonight. And I adore fireworks . . . Look!'

In the centre of the Bay was a large flat-topped raft, or a boat boarded across. On this, several set-pieces were erected. And now rockets soared high, to break into passionate and momentary flower, and fall and die . . . And a thousand throats drew in their breaths sharply as the rockets hissed up, and gave an ecstatic cry as they flowered, and sighed as their spangles blinked into oblivion . . .

Then the fireworks were over and the final preparations were begun, with impatient cries for San Rocca lilting across the water. The boats moved in and out, jockeying for position. Bengal lights flared luridly, illuminating — of all things — a pair of steps at one end of the raft. With shrill cries, a figure was driven up them. There were screams and cat-calls and raucous laughter. A kind of scarecrow he seemed to be, wearing a wide tattered straw hat and a ragged cotton suit. He stood poised at the top of the ladder, watching the crowd hurling good-humoured abuse at him and waving their fists.

Suddenly he spread out his arms and flew downward like a bird, piercing the water with scarcely a splash.

There was an instantaneous roar of pleasure and satisfaction from the crowd. They stamped and yelled and took up the song again more vigorously than hitherto. They jumped about, kissing one another impartially. Their high-pitched excited laughter became increasingly frequent . . . Rattles and streamers filled the air . . . On the quay they began to dance . . . The light craft bobbed and swirled dangerously out in the harbour, their fairy lights tossing and flaring with the movements of the excited crews . . .

Prudence cried: 'Mr. Seal!' Behind her spectacles her eyes were huge and shadowy with fear, and her face was very pale.

'What's the trouble?' he asked.

'He hasn't come up! He dived, and he never came up again.'

'He must have done. It's difficult to see what's going on out there. But those people on the raft are much nearer than we are, they would be bound to have noticed if he had not come up again. Don't worry.'

'They weren't paying any attention. I was.' She was wrestling with the complicated fastening of the painter as she spoke. 'I'm going to look myself. If you don't want to come, you'd better get out now,' she said tersely.

He strained his eyes to a point beyond the raft with its dying Bengal lights, to where the scarecrow had disappeared. And then he saw, floating lazily away, the pale battered hat. He felt a chill of fear run through the pit of his stomach.

Prudence was jabbing furiously at the motor, which gave no more than a surly sputter. Quentin took over and kicked the engine to life.

Most of the fun was over now: the more sober-minded were going home, and the others desired more secluded rioting. The raft trailed slowly back to shore with the skeletons of the feast aboard — the gaunt scaffolding of the set-pieces and the stepladder, stark and gallows-like.

As they passed, Quentin called to them.

'What's become of San Rocca?'

'Dead, dead, dead . . . Good ol' San Rocca, he dead . . . '

Quentin drew in closer and begged them to stop kidding. He was serious. What had really happened to the chap who dived from the ladder?

'Who knows? Dead, perhaps. Come alive next year, perhaps.' Shrieks of mirth.

It was impossible to get any sense out of them. They were drunk with gaiety.

They chugged about in ever widening circles. But there was nothing to be seen but scraps of paper and cigarette ends and banana skins. And the hat. They rescued the hat. Prudence took the battered sodden thing onto her lap. She gave a little whimper.

'I wonder if it would be any use diving down to take a look? It was just about here he disappeared,' said Quentin.

'Oh, what's the use now?' she cried. 'It's too late. And you may even get killed yourself. Please don't ... Oh, this damned place! Nothing but deaths ... '

'We may be mistaken,' he said soothingly. 'Surely one of those people — half-crazed though they were — would have noticed that he never returned? Who was he anyway?'

'Don't you *know*? It was *Boris*!' And she put her face down on the mucky straw hat and wept.

He was so dumbfounded by this remark that he allowed her to cry in silence for quite a while.

The last boats slipped past them. Quentin shut off the engine and let the boat drift on the current out beyond Palm Point. There was a curious unreality about the whole evening to him. Of course it was only natural she should be upset at the sudden and unexpected death of someone she knew.

'Do you love him?' he asked suddenly. 'Is that why you are crying?'

'It's awful. He's had such a rotten life. He's never had a chance. And he never complained. He was brave; he took just what came to hand, good or bad. And to be cut off like that . . . It's heartbreaking.'

'At least his struggles are over now.'

She stared out to sea without answering him, her clenched fist pressed against her mouth.

At last, she said: 'I didn't know I was in love with a man like that. He wasn't even respectable, and he was no longer very young. What was it about him? Half he said I didn't believe, and I never quite trusted him. But that was *my* nastiness, not his. And now it's too late to be anything else.'

Quentin tentatively offered the suggestion that once she had got over the first pain of it, it was to her advantage that there had been no kind of romance between them: there was the less memory to hurt.

He swung the boat around.

'Perhaps we should go back,' he suggested.

'Not yet,' she begged. 'I can't bear the thought of going back. Here, nothing is real yet.'

They lapsed into silence again; broken presently by Quentin wondering aloud how it could have happened. It must be an accident . . .

Prudence snapped onto it. What did he mean, an accident? What *else* could it be?

Nothing at all, he assured her; it was merely the way his thoughts ran nowadays. Two murders already, and she knew the old saying: *Jamais deux sans trois* . . . No more to it than that.

'Two murders already!' she yelped. 'How do you make that out?'

'Well, that is if La Morte *was* murdered.'

This was evidently a new idea to her, and she digested it quietly for a time. She would not be in the least surprised if there was some funny business in connection with Borodin's death. He was a secretive man and never spoke of what he was up to, but she knew that he was mixed up in some pretty queer concerns. Perhaps someone had found him inconvenient to have around and had engineered a clever exit for him. But if it had anything to do with the Jacques family, she was pretty certain she knew who it was. There was only one as spiteful and malevolent as all that; only one capable of that peculiar kind of trickery and treachery. There was no need to mention names, was there?

The romantic outline of Castelnuovo towering above them, silent and dark but for one small, watchful, yellow eye, was a picturesque shape against the night sky.

They became aware of a distant humming sound like a menacing nocturnal bee, gradually increasing in volume; almost before they realised it, a boat without lights hurtled over the horizon and sped out of sight again. The sound died away.

'But what could be her object?' said Quentin thoughtfully, still pursuing the subject.

'She wouldn't need an object, Mr. Seal. She would very likely look on it as an experiment . . . '

From midway between them and the Point, a thin white beam of light spread in a semi-circle across the water — advancing, retreating, moving from side to side, like some great insect's uncanny feeler. It passed over them, returned, quivered, and held their little cockleshell in its dazzling beam, advancing . . . They shaded their eyes and stared back at the hypnotising searchlight, like birds at a snake.

As the boat chugged nearer, a voice hailed them from behind the light. Who were they? What were they doing out in the Bay at night? Their answers were evidently satisfactory, for the other boat suddenly whipped about and made off rapidly into the dark.

'Coastal patrol,' said Prudence. 'What are they doing?'

It occurred to Quentin that someone might have informed them of the missing beachcomber and they might be searching for him, but he chose not to mention it to the girl just then. He intimated that it was getting late, and that bed was not undesirable now. Already the moon was pale with fatigue as she slanted down the sky. He started up the engine and they chugged slowly back.

A little cluster of boats was going ahead of them into the harbour . . . They made fast to the jetty. Quentin climbed out and stooped to help Prudence up. The vociferous excitement farther along was dying down. Three men climbed out of the boats. They walked briskly. On the quayside they overtook and passed the man and girl. Two of the men wore the long-peaked caps of the Coastal Patrol. The one in the middle was hatless. The radiance from the moon was just strong enough for them to recognise him as he passed.

It was Boris Borodin.

He didn't see them, and they were so taken aback that they let him pass without a word, staring after him open-mouthed, as though he were a ghost. Their shadows slipped noiselessly from darkness to darkness, past the long line of palms stiffly lacquered in silver, and out of sight.

'Well, well,' remarked Quentin with kindly scorn. 'We not only had the poor man dead and buried, but had murdered him into the bargain. This is one of those few times when it is a pleasure to be in the wrong.'

The first hint of dawn was freshening the air. A faraway bird chattered raucously. The windless night was full of furtive little rustling sounds. Their footfalls echoed on the dusty road.

They walked to the foot of Jacob's ladder, wrapped in their private thoughts. Wooden shacks were roughly chalked in moonlight against the night, and blossoms carved of white jade hung from the black masses of the trees. The Island was quiet at last . . . the feast of San Rocca was over.

15

Forty-Eight Hours to Go

Prudence, as she stumbled up the dim steps, was under no delusion about what Borodin had been up to. She had suspected him for some time, ever since the night of Raoul's death, when he had swum to shore. But even now she lacked the proof she wanted, that was the maddening part about it. Her heart almost failed her at the thought that she might be too late. She determined not to be beaten; indeed, she could not afford to be beaten. Accordingly, she began to lay her plans . . .

The next morning, as soon as she could escape from her employer, she was down at the Mairie getting permission to visit the prisoner. To her surprise, this was granted quite readily. Perhaps he was not thought sufficiently important to hide.

The Island prison consisted of a group

of square white houses huddling together with their palm-thatched roofs. Boris was sitting in a cell alone, wearing the long yellow canvas jumper and trousers which was the Island convict garb. A dejected figure, with his head in his hands. When the jailer unlocked the cell door, he raised his head languidly, then his eyes widened and a smile quirked his lips.

'Proo-dance!' he exclaimed from his heart. 'How good of you to come . . . ' He stretched out his hands to her eagerly. But before she had time to clasp them in hers, the jailer stepped between them, and monotonously recited the rule that prisoner and visitor must remain an arm's-length apart. Having said his piece, he moved over to the high window and considerately stood with his back to them.

An awkward silence fell. She did not know how to broach what she had to say, and he did not know how much she knew.

'Your new lodgings are fairly comfortable?' she ventured, showing him she was not ashamed of him for being jailed.

'Better than Queenie's,' he rumbled solemnly.

Again a little silence, then: 'I saw you last night. You made a splendid San Rocca. But when you didn't come up again . . . I was terrified. I thought you were drowned.'

'Ah, Proo-dance!'

'But all's well that ends well. I was wrong. I saw you brought back under escort . . . Nothing worse than . . . a little case of . . . smuggling?'

He said nothing.

'My dear, don't look like that,' she said softly. 'Do you think I don't know what was at the back of it? Somebody's skin had to be saved, and no one was likely to bother what happened to you. But there is someone who cares what happens to you. I do. And I mean to make it my business to see that justice is done and that you have a fair deal.'

'For goodness' sake, my little one, do not meddle yourself in this. What happens to me now doesn't matter. I was already lost from the moment I dropped my identity papers into the sea. I have known it all along, and I have only been waiting for the moment, though I am sorry it should interrupt our happy friendship. Does not one of your poets say: 'The best of friends must part'? We must just be resigned to fate.'

'Don't be so gutless, Boris,' she said vigorously. 'If I say I can help you, it means I can. All I want to know is, who — who is hiding behind you?'

He grimaced at her and nodded to the jailer. 'You will help me by getting my throat slit from ear to ear.'

'This is no time for chivalry or anything of that sort. Consider me,' she pleaded, 'as well as yourself.'

'It is sweet of you, darling, and I am very touched. But now let us talk of other things, please.'

Prudence sighed. 'Is there anything you want? Books? A lawyer?'

'Only some cigarettes, if you can spare them.'

She emptied out her case onto the tree-stump that was clamped to the floor, serving as a rough seat.

'That's all I have on me, but you shall have some more tomorrow.'

'I think my trial will come quite soon,'

he warned her calmly. 'The next sitting, they expect: tomorrow, or the day after.'

'So soon?' Her heart sank.

'There's no reason to postpone it, my dear. The case will be quite plain sailing. I haven't a leg to stand on.'

The jailer came towards them rattling his keys. She wanted to say something to comfort him, but out of the desperate jumble came only: 'I shall see you again.'

The only person whose advice she dared seek was Mr. Seal. He might be able to think up some way to help her, although she would have to guard her tongue that she did not let slip too much.

'I can't help you unless I know what he was doing,' he said sternly.

'Gun-running, of course. What did you imagine he was doing — picking daisies? But don't get funny ideas, Mr. Seal. I *know* he's innocent. I don't mean that he didn't know what cargo he was trying to run. I hold no brief for him as far as that goes. But he's shielding someone else. He was only the hired man; the real criminal is hidden away somewhere. Boris is just an adventurer on the rocks, ready to take any risks in order to earn his bread. He's a victim of circumstance, but that's no reason why he should be victimised. I don't know what sort of horror they can inflict on him legally in this place, but sooner or later I'll get whoever's at the back of this. Boris is shielding the person now, but I shall find out. But there's no time to spare!'

'Miss Whitaker,' said Quentin reproachfully, 'you've known about this for some time now. You should have told me before.'

'Not *known*, only suspected,' she admitted guiltily. 'And only since the night of Raoul's murder, when he tried to land in the creek. I'm sure he had no idea what had happened, but he guessed that something was wrong, and what could he do? He couldn't float around indefinitely — he wouldn't dare, for fear of the Coastal Patrollers. He scuttled the whole thing, as far out as he dared go, and went overboard himself. I saw him swim in, and judging by the state he arrived in, he must have swum about two miles. No wonder he was downhearted, having to report the loss of boat and cargo, knowing that he was not likely to be paid for that little expedition. And on top of that, his papers . . . '

'You think it's a regular thing, then? Been going on for some time?'

'Perhaps,' she said cautiously.

'I see,' he mused. 'You think some kind of coup is being worked on? Insurrection, or revolution perhaps, leading to civil war? Or just nasty troublemaking and racketeering?'

She shrugged. If she knew more, as he suspected, she wasn't going to talk.

He saw now that the feast of San Rocca had been deliberately chosen as a night when a boat's activities might well pass unnoticed among so many other absurd antics. The gun-runners could be excused for expecting the Coastal Patrollers to be less vigilant on such a night of junketing.

It seemed that a good swimmer was always chosen for the role of San Rocca! It was necessary for him to stay underwater for quite a time — long enough, anyhow, to swim to a dark and empty boat anchored a little way off, unnoticeable amid the illuminated flotilla.

Once aboard, it was simplicity itself to drop the cable and drift on the current beyond sight and earshot. Once out of the Bay, Borodin could start up the engine and set his course for the boat he was to meet, whatever it was — probably sailing from Venezuela, with its inflammatory cargo. The light craft would load up and wave a silent farewell. It was possible that even if the Patrollers had spotted him they would not have caught him, had not his heavy load forced him to reduce speed. Perhaps it was chance, or perhaps they had been tipped a warning; however it was, they had spread a cunning net for him, the Patrol boats closing in like compass points.

Boris was to be charged on the following day during the general session. And Quentin agreed to go with Prudence, who was determined to be there whether Miss Brown liked it or not. Just then, she didn't give a damn for Miss Brown.

The outside of the law-courts was an ugly nineteenth-century Gothic, but inside, some of the chambers had a queer effective dignity, created by the bare whitewashed walls and the high-backed ebony benches like church pews. Before the court sat, an attendant came in and pulled a screen of rush-matting across the open glass roof to keep off the worst of the sun.

The small courtroom was barely half-full. The day's sitting was before Justice Jacques. He swept in through the door at the far end. He looked very grand and stately in his flowing black silk gown with lace at his throat and wrists. Because of the heat, wigs were only worn on ceremonial occasions. Instead, he wore a small red hat not unlike a cardinal's. With a flourish, he sat himself behind a carved desk on a dais, and clasped his hands together till absolute silence was restored.

The session began.

Both Quentin and Prudence had overlooked that it was held in French. He knew enough to get by with in a general way, but this queer Island dialect was beyond him. Prudence was in a little better case because she had been on the

Island long enough to pick up a generous smattering.

The cases were dull enough anyway — money owing on monthly bills, a theft of petty cash, and one or two cases they could not make out.

Then Boris Borodin was led in, wearing prison garb. He looked calm enough, but the need of a shave did nothing to improve his appearance. He was marched with quick rough movements behind a high wooden rail with a serrated top. There was gabbling. Then: '*Prisonnier! Attention!*' And the indictment was read out.

The prisoner was charged with attempting absolute contraband, i.e. the running-in of firearms with nefarious intent.

'*Eh bien!*' said Justice Jacques. 'Proceed. What is the prisoner's name and nationality?'

The prosecutor admitted that legally the prisoner possessed neither, owing to the absence of all identity papers. The prisoner claimed that he was a White Russian, born 1902, in the province of the Ukraine, and that his name was Boris Borodin. The prosecutor shrugged. It *might* be true. On the other hand, his description agreed equally well with that of a certain jewel-thief, wanted for murder, who had escaped from Dutch Guiana three months earlier, where he had been imprisoned by the Dutch authorities.

Prudence's hands were hot and sticky. In the name of heaven, was that man trying to frame him? She was a coward not to have offered to give evidence for the defence, because she knew it might harm her in her work, and would be unforgivable in the eyes of her boss. But if there was going to be any hanky-panky, she would still get up without premeditation and interfere.

But she did not need to just then. The prosecutor's droning voice was cut short in the middle of reading out the description of the man wanted in Dutch Guiana from the police records.

The judge interrupted. 'That scarcely seems relevant at present, Maitre Faro. Kindly resume your accusation.'

He rustled the papers and continued, describing the enormity of the prisoner's offences. He called the gallant Patrollers to testify. They identified the prisoner as the man they had caught in the small seas with a cargo of firearms, unspecified.

Boris listened to it all with an expressionless face. At last he was allowed to speak. He was defending himself.

To begin with, he admitted that he had been in the boat carrying contraband cargo, just as the Patrollers had said, but their mistake was in thinking that he was bringing it to Apostle Island. Such was not his destination. Doubtless their error was excusable, because in his efforts to shake them off his track he had doubled back under the lee of the Island. But how did that prove it to be the natural end of his journey? Had they seen him start out on his expedition or pick up his cargo? No; for if they had, they would know that he had actually left the Island with the munitions aboard.

Jacques frowned severely and demanded to be told where the prisoner had obtained these articles on the

Island. But that the prisoner firmly declined to state. Nor would he say for where they were bound. His lips were sealed. That would do him little good, they told him; a free confession warranted a free pardon. But he shook his head and, glancing across to the dim benches where Mr. Seal sat, replied that he could never be a stool-pigeon.

The judge glanced about the court, cleared his throat, and began the summing-up and sentence.

As the prisoner obstinately and misguidedly refused to reveal the true facts and so assist the course of justice, little was known. But it was fairly obvious that the miserable wretch before them was a mere pawn in the elaborate game of some more mischievous mind. Plainly he possessed neither the means nor ability for such enterprises. It had therefore to be taken into consideration that the real criminal had eluded them, leaving only the tool in their hands. Who it was might never be known, but this unfortunate escapade might be sufficient to frighten them from attempting further activities of that sort. Nor could they know that the cargo was not intended for the Island, but came *from* the Island. The Patrollers' story had to be taken into account, too. It was altogether very unsatisfactory. It was not even known who the prisoner was. One thing alone was clear. The prisoner had a bad character, was the worst type of ne'er-do-well. He was not the kind of person they wanted on Apostle, and in his opinion the sooner they got rid of him the better. On account of his suspicious lack of identification papers alone, he was liable to from three to six months' imprisonment, but Jacques saw no reason why Island taxes should go to support him, a foreigner — probably a Bolshevik. Taking every consideration into account, he had come to the conclusion that the sooner the prisoner was excluded from the Island economy, the better. He therefore would make out a deportation order for him to leave Apostle Island within forty-eight hours of notice being given, with the warning of immediate arrest and imprisonment should he be discovered after the expiry of the notice, or should he return to the Island at some future date.

Borodin said nothing, but his hands gripped the spiky wood of the rail before him for support. A uniformed mulatto man tapped his shoulder, jerking his head sideways in the direction the prisoner should be moving. But Boris ignored him.

'M-Monsieur!' he stammered. 'How am I to leave without money or papers? And who will give me asylum? Only forty-eight hours . . . it isn't possible, sir, in the time . . . I beg you to reconsider . . . '

But the judge was not even listening. He rapped his gavel sharply on the echoing wood. And the prisoner was removed. The court was cleared for the next case.

Prudence moved out into the harsh sunlight and stood blinking stupidly. Her heart was wrung with pity for Boris's predicament. In all fairness, she recognised that Jacques had been lenient as well as just; it was hardly his fault that his mercy was not really merciful at all. She wondered what would become of Boris, and whether there was any way out for him.

Mr. Seal, at her side, suddenly remarked that he intended to go up to Jacques' house on the following day to hold an important meeting, at which he hoped everyone would be present. It would have to be tomorrow, before Boris left the community. Would Prudence be sure to be there?

She nodded vaguely. She would certainly do her best; but right then she had an important engagement . . . it had escaped her memory until that instant . . . with Father Xavier . . .

'Wait a minute, Miss Whitaker,' he called after her. 'I'll come with you. I want to speak to him about this meeting. He must be there too.'

'What's the meeting about? Is it anything to do with — ' She looked suddenly frightened. 'Do you think you've discovered Raoul's murderer?'

'It's about time I did,' he parried. 'I'm sure I'm not the only one who thinks so, either . . . But don't look so alarmed, Miss Whitaker, or I shall suspect *you*, and

I'm sure you're much too nice to have such very unpleasant habits.'

'I was thinking,' she said slowly, 'that the murderer will have to be tried according to French law, won't they? They regard you as guilty until you prove your innocence. What kind of justice is that?'

'I dare say it works all right for them. Murder — real murder, not euthanasia or anything of that sort — takes so little account of justice towards its victim, that it deserves little justice in return.'

'I agree, so long as there is no possible likelihood of a miscarriage of justice.' She licked her lips nervously. 'But that so rarely happens, doesn't it? Look at that stupid mess-up today. No attempt has been made to find the real culprit, and they admitted frankly that Boris was not the one.'

'All the same, he got off very lightly, my dear, considering that there can have been little doubt that the cargo's destination *was* Apostle. It was very clever of him to have thought of that way out of it,' said Quentin consolingly.

'He's quick-witted and sensible. If he'd ever had half a chance . . . '

'Oh well, you've always had a soft spot for him,' said Mr. Seal slyly, 'ever since the night you tried to prevent Jacques recognising him, with the cargo that he subsequently tipped overboard. At least, that was the first I knew of it.'

'Yes,' said Prudence thoughtfully. 'How clever of you, Mr. Seal . . . I've always had a soft spot for Boris.'

Father Xavier was out when they arrived at his bleached cabin. Miss Whitaker prepared herself to wait for him, but Quentin had much to do, and scrawled a hasty note which he folded intricately and handed to the native servant.

'Till tomorrow then, Miss Whitaker,' he reminded her.

'I hope so,' she said gravely. 'In any case, thank you for helping me immensely . . . You've made me see quite clearly what I have to do.'

On his way back through Wigtown, Mr. Seal paused outside a shop in the Rue de l'Isle de la Victoire, that had a window full of yellow-back paper books and fly-swatters, and in one corner a large, gaudily-coloured map of the island. It was expensive, but he bought it nevertheless, for even if it was of no use to him in the purpose for which he wanted it, it made a quaint souvenir.

He also bought a postcard with an artificial view, penned a brief message on its blank surface, and addressed it to the Foleys' villa on Palm Point.

It only remained to find out at what time Borodin was released from jail and collect him on his way out. Then he could set to work in earnest in an attempt to get the last threads neatly tied together before the approaching meeting.

But it was not till late that night that he was able to retire to his room. With a bottle of 'inspiration' and a siphon beside him, he sprawled at his ease on the bed and assembled the chaotic notes he had made as the case progressed.

When dawn came, the best of the bottle was gone, and the big copper ashtray was full. The bed was littered with sheets of paper scribbled over and scratched through. Behind the grubby mosquito netting, Mr. Seal slept, oblivious of the insects' triumphant song at the proximity of so much defenceless flesh . . .

16

Daylight

Even in the sullen afternoon heat, the tower-room was comparatively cool. They drifted into it thankfully, one by one. First, Miss Brown, Orlando on her arm. She plumped down regally in a spacious wooden armchair, greeting Mr. Seal with an abstracted nod. A few minutes later, Boris Borodin came in in a half-hearted sort of way, his unease more on account of his surroundings than the situation, but he carried it off quite well. Then Father Xavier arrived, his round brown face running with sweat. He greeted everyone with professional brightness, and at once sat down beside Borodin and entered into conversation with him.

With the arrival of Mr. and Mrs, Foley, the whole atmosphere changed from one of guarded wariness to a social gathering.

They evidently were not aware of what was expected of them. They evinced some surprise at the company, but decided that if the party was to be a quiet one, so much the better; Foley had not been out anywhere yet since his arrest; it would be more discreet for him to slide gently back into society like this.

When Jacques came in, somewhat preoccupied but full of dignity, Hattie patted the chair next to hers invitingly and he seated himself beside her.

Mr. Seal raised his head from the paper he was writing on and stared round at them searchingly. Then he sighed and laid down his pen.

'Well, if we're all here, we may as well begin,' he remarked.

Borodin said: 'Miss Whitaker is not here.'

'Twenty minutes' grace ought to be enough for anybody.' Mr. Seal shrugged. 'I don't think we need wait.' He glanced around.

'I suppose you realise why I've asked you to come here? It concerns this murder in which we have all, one way or another, been involved. You know, of course, that I was asked to co-operate in solving this unpleasant crime. I did not want to undertake it. I had only the haziest idea how to go about things, and as time passed I seemed to make no progress. However, lately things have begun to clarify somewhat.

'Since you have all suffered from the crime, and since you must all be interested in it to some extent, I thought it only fair to put the latest developments before you to see whether you reached the same conclusions as myself.

'But first, I must warn you that I shall be obliged to reveal all manner of things that individually you would wish kept secret. The best thing will be if you make up your minds in advance to forget immediately anything that may be said this afternoon about anybody else. If at any time anyone feels offended at what I say, I beg him or her to remember that a particularly vile crime has been committed and our one aim should be to solve it. Agreed?'

'No,' said Evelyn Foley smartly, and

stood up, angrily pulling on her fashion-
able net mittens. 'I consider we've been
brought here under false pretences. I
would never have come here to be
insulted . . . I'll not put up with it, for
one. Come, Johnny, we're going. *He* can't
stop us.'

'Of course I can't stop you,' said Mr.
Seal mildly. 'Go, by all means. It was in
fairness to you that I asked you here.
After all, there is no way in which you can
stop me saying anything I choose about
you and your husband, but I thought it
might be to your interest to hear what I
am going to say . . . Just as you like,
however.'

She glared at him furiously, and then
capitulated wordlessly with a sulky face.
She sat down again.

'To begin with,' Mr, Seal resumed, 'my
initial introduction to the family was one
of horror. There seemed to be something
sinister, even uncanny, about Madame
Jacques' death, something instinctively
queer in the general atmosphere. I had
nothing special in mind, but I just wasn't
satisfied.

'Then Raoul Jacques was found dead in the bathing-hut by the creek, and Mr. Jacques asked me to help, as I have already mentioned. Raoul was killed at night, probably between nine and ten o'clock. Death was instantaneous and the body was not moved afterwards. In other words, he was killed where he lay, on the narrow bunk beneath the window. And in confirmation of that fact, the wall above the bunk was slightly flecked with blood. He was half-undressed and lying face-downward. The clothes which he or another had removed had been flung-earelessly on the floor. He might have been stripping for-a moonlight bathe, but for the fact that there was no costume or towel. The cushion beneath his head had been dragged away and left on the floor. There was only one door and one window. And the hut's sole illumination must have come from the pale moon.

'I think that is all that struck me as important at the time. Except that, after the body had been removed, I found a hairpin at the head of the bunk. It belonged to Mrs. Foley, and she admitted that she had been there. She had gone there at his request, and she had left before the murder, she said — naturally. I accepted that statement provisionally. But later she confessed that she had been in the hut at the actual moment when Raoul was murdered — an amazing thing to say! Since there were no witnesses she could call in her defence, it was tantamount to a confession of guilt. Not only that, but her next statement was more incredible still. She had neither seen nor heard the murderer, and she had not become aware of the fatal act until it was too late. Imagine to yourselves that there were already two people confined in a space eight feet by four, and yet one of them was killed by a third person, unwitnessed. It savoured of magic. If she were telling the truth — and, to a certain extent, she was — one could only presume that she must have been unconscious or in some trance-state.'

He stole a sideways glance at her as she gazed abstractedly out of the deep-set window.

'She faked up some kind of a tale

which she thought might satisfy me, but a fiction-writer's whole craft is in the spinning of convincing lies, and he readily acquires the knack of detecting the more improbable inventions of other people. She would have liked me to believe that she was the victim of an attempted rape.' Mr. Seal grimaced sourly. 'I didn't even bother to pretend I believed her. I soon found out that there was more to it than that. There was evidence of gifts exchanged: two of which at least were not customary gifts between a married woman and a young boy. She had given him a silver cigarette-case, and he had given her a handsome pair of diamond-and-emerald clips. Clearly there was some intimate relationship between them which had probably been established for some time. Presumably there were no claims of fidelity on either side, but that does not entirely obviate jealousy . . . '

He was aware of Jacques' sombre expression as he continued: 'Raoul had all the makings of a cad as far as women were concerned. He was fickle and lacking in sympathy. What had he in him to attract a woman of Mrs. Foley's type? Nothing beyond his undeniable good looks, his sensual ardour . . . and, above all, his youth. To a woman of her age, his youth was probably his greatest charm; he must have represented to her the last of romance. I don't suppose she meant to fall in love with him; all she wanted was to snatch at the passing bliss. Imagine the disaster of falling in love with a boy like Raoul! The hopeless fires of jealousy she must have felt consuming her, time and time again! To add to her difficulties, Foley became suspicious, and went so far as to forbid Raoul the house, and indeed all association between them. Here, then, was an opportunity for Raoul to break away. He had a cowardly nature; and besides, he was tired of her scenes. Perhaps there was another woman who was being importunate, too. Still, one or two meetings were dangerously contrived between them. Probably the disused bathing-hut was his idea, though whether they had used it before it is hard to say. They went there at a time convenient to them both, when she knew her husband would be working late and when he would not be under his family's surveillance. As a double precaution, she told the servants she was going to bed early, and let them go. So there was no one to see her steal out to the rendezvous with her lover.'

'Look here, sir, I don't care for your tone,' said Mr. Foley, suddenly waking up. 'The whole thing is a fabrication from beginning to end. I admit there was a kind of flirtatious friendship between them. I thought it was unhealthy and I didn't hesitate to show my disapproval pretty plainly. That was the end of it . . . I don't know what your object is in trying to blacken a woman's name like this, but no one but an out-and-out rotter would do such a thing, and I'm not going to sit by and hear my wife being slandered. To say that kid was my wife's lover, is an insult to us both.'

'I appreciate it's a rotten position for you,' said Mr. Seal sympathetically. 'But it's useless to take up that attitude now. You may as well let me finish. You know your wife better than we do, I suppose; a

317

passionate woman, illogical and immoral. Do you find it impossible to believe that in a fit of ungovernable jealousy she stabbed a man in the back?'

Mrs. Foley faced round at that and raised trembling hand to her mouth. Her eyes were frightened.

'I didn't do it,' she croaked. 'You must be mad. I know no more about it than I told you. All right, I did love him, just as you said. I couldn't leave him alone. I only lived when I was with him. So, you see, it isn't possible that *in any circumstances* I could have — killed him. I might have killed myself, I suppose, if he'd got tired of me. But in his own way, I believe he loved me. I know he wasn't faithful — how could I reproach him for that? Neither was I — but he really was fond of me, and proud of my being his mistress. Oh, we had scenes. I hated to see him carrying on under my nose with — with anyone . . . his dirty old aunt — ' She shot Hattie a venomous glance, which was received with a malicious cackle. ' — or that secretary bitch. He always pretended it was solely in order to put people off the scent, and that used to make me wilder than anything. But we didn't have a row that night, I swear it. I loved him. I never did it!' She hid her tears with her two hands . . . Foley stared gloomily at the floor.

'My dear Mrs. Foley, I never said you did. I only asked your husband whether he could believe such a thing of you. And he certainly defended you a little overzealously. However, there's no harm in that . . . No, I didn't mean that you had killed him, only that you *could* have done. No, Raoul was killed while you were tranced in the very act of ecstatic love. You were only conscious of him, and not until Death's thrust had slackened his body did you become aware that anything was wrong.'

With a pained expression, Jacques said: 'This is extremely sordid, Mr. Seal; is it really necessary?'

'I agree, sir. It's an outrage,' exclaimed Mr. Foley.

Mr. Seal sighed. 'You can't suppose that I have any pleasure in these details. I am merely making the position clear to everyone. I will pass over it as quickly as I can, I assure you. If you will allow me to proceed without further interruptions, we will get this over with faster . . .

'As soon as Mrs. Foley realised what was wrong, her one thought, rather ignobly, was for herself. How could she get away without detection? If she was to remain unconnected with this crime, the sooner she made her getaway the better. After all, if she stayed, there was nothing she could do. It did not require any special knowledge to tell her life was extinct. To unlock and open the door she had to use the key, and in her distracted state it seemed to her the safest thing to take it away with her. So she fled. I surmise that she purposely left the door open, hoping that the body would thus be discovered sooner. That was a sop to her conscience for not sounding an immediate alarm. When she got home she tried to put the whole thing right out of her mind. Her behaviour must in no way deviate from the norm. The key was an encumbrance to her. If it should be found, it would instantly link her up with the crime. In a kind of panic, she thrust it into a pocket of her husband's suit. Then she went to bed . . . I wonder if she slept?'

'It's an interesting bit of scandal,' Hattie commented drily, 'but I still can't see where it is leading us . . . '

'*Pazienza!*' he counselled. 'You are all very fidgety today. I'm explaining it as fast as I can. I should have thought you would all grasp the implications of this story at once.'

'You mean,' said Father Xavier, 'that if the lad was not killed by Mrs. Foley, the person who had most reason to do it was — ' He paused and moistened his lips.

'John Foley? Exactly. He had already warned them both, and made no bones about what he would do to him if he ever found them together again. He said that in front of several people, including myself. How much he suspected, and how much he actually knew, it is hard to gauge now. But if he found out about his wife's carryings-on, it would need a psychologically sounder man than he to withstand the shock of pain and humiliation. Here then was someone who had motive *and* opportunity: it would have been easy enough to escape from his work, for there was no one to oversee him; and he came up to Miss Brown's soon after — looking rather bedraggled, I remember. He could also have obtained the weapon; he was at the priest's house the day before, and the weapon came from there. Whether he stole it with malice aforethought, or whether it was some subconscious prompting, we cannot judge. But in French law, any man would be forgiven for stabbing his wife's lover in the back, finding them *in flagrante*.

'Those were the conclusions reached by the police. But I was not altogether content with this reasoning. Although he was the most likely person, with a strong motive, I could not see murder as his natural reaction to infidelity. It's not English logic. For, whatever else he is besides, Johnny Foley is an Englishman — ' Foley looked gratified. ' — and stabbing a chap in the back without warning is contrary to the inflexible laws of good form. Only if one could somehow circumvent those two facts would I wholeheartedly support the case against Foley.

Jacques inspected the cheroots in the olive-wood box on the table as he spoke. 'In any case, Mr. Foley has been imprisoned and released. Can we not take it for granted that he is innocent . . . of this particular crime, anyway?'

'It narks you to think of him robbing your sister-in-law all these years undiscovered, doesn't it?' Mr. Seal smiled. 'I wonder how much he has salted away? I thought from the first time I met him that he had a very good reason for living here; he was so vehement in his dislike of it. What was the name by which you were known to the police in England, Mr. Foley?' he asked drily.

Johnny looked haughty and indignant at the same time. 'I suppose you think that's funny,' he said.

'On the contrary. But never mind — it has little or nothing to do with the subject in hand. The point I want to make is that I had my eye on someone just as likely for the part of murderer as you. Someone who, like you, had access to the weapon, and had equal motive and opportunity. Moreover — and this was the thing that appealed to me — it linked up with the death of Raoul's mother, which had been preying on my subconscious all this while. This new suspect required a reorientation of the crime — or, rather, the two crimes. Because, this way, it was the first crime that counted; the second one was almost accidental, a covering of the tracks through fright. Motive in this first case was neither love nor jealousy, but money. La Morte left her money to the Church. We may presume that Father Xavier knew all about it. He knew therefore that the money was to come to him some day: is it inconceivable that, by some Jesuitical line of reasoning, he might have seen fit to hasten that occasion . . . ? Now, for goodness' sake, do all of you try to contain your thoughts and emotions about this. I'm not saying that he did it, it just seemed to me a possibility — perhaps even a probability, because he was clearly not telling me all he knew; part of the truth he was holding back.

'But the second murder was a bungled affair. The murderer had made a stupid mistake this time. He must have been badly frightened. The first death, however it was encompassed, was cleverly done, and had been passed off quite easily as misadventure due to negligence. And if it had not been for my interference, it might not have gone as far as that, even. The second death looked like a hasty attempt to stop a blabbing mouth.

'I reasoned in this way . . . Our hypothesis being for the moment that the good Father was responsible for La Morte's death, supposing Raoul had found this out, what would he have done? He would certainly have done his best to turn it to account. He might have insisted on the money being returned to him, for he continued to regard it as rightfully his. Or he might have warned the priest that he knew, and threatened him with the police. But, knowing what I do now, the thought that leaps to my mind is that Raoul would have tried to blackmail him. Be that as it may, there would not be a moment to lose if Father Xavier's secret was to remain secret. Raoul must die, and die at once.

'In an impromptu act of this kind, it was not surprising to find that he used the first weapon that came to hand — the stiletto he used for paper-cutting. That did strike me as a little too jaunty and careless to be true, I admit. In books, criminal characters are made enormously crafty — if not, there would be no conflict — but there is no accounting for the stupidity of people in real life; I find the most intelligent, the most far-seeing and practical people often unthinkingly do things that for sheer dottiness take a lot of beating. Also, he might even have thought it out as a bit of deliberate cunning to fox us. Perhaps half the threats Raoul was credited with having hurled at the poor Father's head were invented by him as a blind. One thing that puzzled me was how the priest could have known he would find the boy at the bathing-hut at that time of night. That savoured of omniscience — unless he had arranged to meet him there on some pretext or other.

But, directly one accepted that suggestion, it brought a whole fresh crop of difficulties in its train. I hesitated uncertainly.'

Father Xavier folded his little brown paws together.

'I had no idea I was ever in such danger,' he said calmly. 'You know what really happened. It serves me right for my own dishonesty; I deserve to have been taken for a murderer. I thought it was suicide, and I should have said so, and the more I tried to hide my thoughts about it, the guiltier I felt. I did feel in some way responsible for the poor soul's death. I should have saved her; I should have known. I was her father confessor. Yes, I blame myself, Mr. Seal, not you.'

Borodin, who had been fidgeting for some minutes, now leant forward with a puzzled frown.

'Mr. Seal, where is Proo — Miss Whitaker? Surely she should be here by now?'

'Surely she should,' he agreed. 'I wonder what can have detained her?'

'Should I go and look for her, do you

think? Something might have happened to her — an accident . . . ' he said deeply.

'I don't see what good you would do by that. Unless you knew where to look.'

Boris hesitated and looked at the other furtively.

'I do not know where to look, but I think I do know what she is looking for.'

'I see. But why are you worried? Surely, when she has found what she wants, she will come along. What should have happened to her?'

He rubbed his hand over his bald head.

'I feel responsible. It was through me she learned of this — thing. If anything has happened — ' He made a despairing gesture.

'I don't see there is anything to work yourself up about so far,' said Mr. Seal, with amused condescension. 'She's certain to turn up soon. If not, we'll all go and hunt for her. You are both inclined to be overanxious about one another . . . Remember the time she swore you were drowned?'

'I do,' said Boris. 'It was the night I was caught gun-running. That's what I mean.'

There was a significance in his tone which did not escape Quentin, though he could not comprehend its nature.

Therefore, he shrugged vaguely, and said: 'Let us continue with this exposition, if you don't mind . . . I was saying that, having once found a link between the two deaths, I was reluctant to let it go. The fact that they occurred in one family within a few weeks of one another seemed of great significance to me. On the other hand, it narrowed down the range of suspects considerably. There were few people who could benefit by Madame Jacques' death. I remembered Mrs. Foley's cattish remark about Mr. Jacques. Was there any warrant for it, I wondered? But, try as I might, I could find no hint of scandal in relation to him. His life appeared to be blameless. He was supposed to be devoted to his wife, and certainly everything contrived to give that impression. I shouldn't imagine that it was easy to live a double life in a small community like this; if that was what he was doing, he was managing his affairs more cleverly than most. I had to repudiate the idea.

'What other reason was there for a man to rid himself of a useless wife? Money. True, it wasn't a large sum that she left, but women have been killed for far smaller amounts than that, if the need was great enough. Suppose he were badly in debt, for instance? But I could find no proof, again, that he was in debt at all, beyond the simple everyday sort of bills. Nothing outstanding. Dead-end again. Yet I remembered a certain evening — the day of the funeral, to be exact — when he had thought himself unseen and unheard, and he gave way to an instant's uncontrollable emotion. I was on the terrace above him, as he cried out unhappily, as though in protest, something like: 'What was the use? Julia! Julia! How shall I manage now?' Then he heard me and I slid out of sight into the shadow, but I did not forget. It occurred to me that his little speech was capable of a different interpretation than its face-value. It might mean that his efforts had been in vain, and that after all he was unable to work things as he wanted.

Remember, he had just learnt the truth about his wife's will. Still, I thought, surely he would have found out about that beforehand. It seems a little too haphazard. And then the one who had been really angry about the money was not he, but Raoul. Raoul was the one who was so cruelly disappointed about it, and so savagely bitter; just as he was the one who plotted so wildly to get the money back from the priest. Again, if the money had been left to Raoul and not Jacques, and my earlier reasoning was correct, that would justify the boy's murder. As it was, what reason had Jacques to kill his own son?'

'He was a bad boy,' said Jacques, with a sad half-smile, 'but not as bad as that.'

Mr. Seal turned to Hattie.

'You knew just what kind of a bad boy he was, didn't you, Miss Brown? You encouraged him in all kinds of wickedness, didn't you? You believe in wickedness for its own sake, I know . . . ' And without waiting for her to answer he continued, addressing the others. 'Miss Whitaker — among others — used to

331

warn me. She had nothing specific against Miss Brown that she cared to mention, but she didn't trust her and she begged me not to. One thing I found out quite soon was that Miss Brown practised witchcraft. How much she believed in it, I don't know, but I think the main thing was that it gave her a tremendous sense of power. And not only over other stupid wretched human beings, but over the very powers of darkness themselves. She liked to frighten Miss Whitaker and see her squirm; she tried to sap her will by hypnotism, but Miss Whitaker had a pretty shrewd guess what she was up against. It tickled her to work against Father Xavier, and over this she was hand in glove with her nephew — until, in his opinion, she went too far in witchcraft by trying to kill the priest. He had already had one severe heart attack, when Raoul found out its origin, and there was an almighty row between the two of them in which he threatened her with exposure and she swore to get even with him.

'I wondered whether La Morte had been killed by sorcery, and if so how one could possibly find it out — and prove it. How had the woman died, anyway? Was it a coincidence, or was she . . . helped over the brink of eternity? How could she have been killed in a way that left no trace — leaving witchcraft out of account for the time being? She could easily have been smothered, of course. But someone would have had to do it. And in the ordinary way she was never left alone for long enough to be harmed. Had the murderer planned and then awaited his opportunity? But how could he know that on that particular day everyone was going to fail in their duty? Unless it was all prearranged, which I did not believe. That would have necessitated accomplices, and the whole thing savoured of flawless simplicity; therein lay its brilliance. Then how? Had Miss Brown in some dark way mesmerised her animals, or trained them to such a pitch of obedience that one of them could have been made to smother the defenceless woman? Or was the business with the cat merely a red herring?

'But then again, however she contrived

the death of her sister, why should she kill her nephew? She was rather fond of him, he was good company, he flattered her immoderately and she was proud of him. Not to mention the fact that I did not even have a motive for her to have killed her sister. Revenge? What harm could she ever have done, except perhaps in the remote past? Money? Absurd, for Hattie had *far* more money than Julia, and would have no reason to suppose that she would have left the money to her rather than to her son or her husband. Then why . . . ? For that matter, although she might well have killed her sister, I could not for the life of me see how either she or Jacques could have had the opportunity to kill the boy. I was there that night, and I subsequently timed those infernal steps up and down . . . It was beyond the bounds of possibility — unless they flew.' He shrugged his shoulders. 'There I was, back at the beginning again, with two separate crimes on my hands. I was almost despairing at my own uncertainty when a new clue was handed to me on a platter, as it were, in the shape of a manikin: an absurd, unskilfully-made, waxen figure. Miss Whitaker, who gave it to me, believed it was intended to harm Mr. Jacques, whom it was meant to represent. But it was not necessarily so. She had a misconception of the use of obeah: one did not hope to harm or benefit a person by means of it, it only helped to give one *power* over that person, and once the person was in one's power it became comparatively simple to dominate them in any desired direction. Miss Brown wished to acquire power over her brother-in-law, then, that much we knew; exactly for what purpose she wanted it, we did not yet know. Later on, I learnt of it from her own lips. I don't think she meant to tell me, but she was in such a state of happy agitation that *someone* had to be told, and I happened to be the person on the spot. Even then, she had enough self-control to do no more than hint at it, but she admitted that after half a lifetime's struggle she was coming within grasping distance of her goal. Is it any wonder that she was excited? I understood, then, when I glimpsed the remote design that had formed the pattern for the whole of her life afterwards . . . a pattern based on a combination of jealousy and love, frustrated love. I saw it all: the beautiful young sister, petted and admired — in contrast to the other, older by several years, physically unattractive, neurotically streaked with brilliance. She falls in love with the handsome Creole, and he is half-captivated — or appears to be — by her wit and her wealth. But then the young beauty turns up and it is all over. There is no longer any hesitation. The two of them fall madly in love; they are made for one another. Now, if Jacques had rejected Hattie in the ordinary way, it would have been a blow to her pride, but in time she would have got over it. To lose him to her sister was an unforgivable slight from both of them. She found herself far more desperately in love with him than before. She wanted him with all her mind and heart and body. She had never been seriously thwarted in her life until then. Because of that, when she found that no storms or cries made the slightest difference, she determined on revenge. Or perhaps that is not quite right; it was not so much revenge she desired, as to get her own way, however long she might have to wait for it. Here was a motive, a live profound motive, for her to have killed her sister. And then, on the day of which I'm speaking, she suggested — oh, ever so slightly — that in the not-too-distant future her aim might be achieved and marriage with Jacques attained.

'I knew then I had no time to lose, no time for leisurely cogitation; I had to act. One of the points that had hindered me by its obscurity up till then was exactly how La Morte had been killed — if killed she was. Remember, she was alone at the time. For the hundredth time I went over the events of that afternoon in my mind's eye. Suddenly one of the harmless facts jumped out at me. Before the nurse had gone out, she had given her patient an injection. Nothing wrong with that. There was the box still by the bedside, half-used, with the empty spaces neatly dated. No, nothing wrong if that had actually been the injection given; but suppose another had been substituted! Wouldn't the nurse have noticed it, though? Not if the substitution had not been that of the phial, but of *the liquid in the phial*. The phials were unusually big, made to contain two cubic centimetres, and they had self-sealing rubber tops instead of the more customary thin glass necks to be filed through. The entire contents of the phial were not necessarily to be used at once, and directly the hypodermic needle was withdrawn, the rubber contracted again and sealed the contents hermetically. It would have been quite easy for any one used to a hypodermic syringe to withdraw the contents — and, by the same means, refill the phial with a more lethal liquid.

'So much was hypothesis, and I had to know what this lethal liquid was that left no trace in her body. I needed proof . . . And there *was* something to hand in the house: something quite harmless in itself, but an overdose of which would prove fatal. And, unless one knew what to look for, it would leave no trace, for it made no deposit but altered by absorption ... I hoped to goodness it would not be too late to find this organic change in the cadaver, having regard for the climate.' He cleared his throat. 'I don't think I need go into that. The important thing is that I was in time. And the doctor told me that the essential quality that should be missing from the blood — if I was right in my surmise — *was* missing. There was my proof. I no longer had any doubts whatsoever.' He stared round at their faces slowly, as if to surprise a reaction out of them.

'*The characteristic lacking in the blood,*' he said, spacing his words with careful emphasis, '*was sugar!* La Morte's blood was entirely devoid of sugar, without which it is as impossible to live as it is with too much. Someone in the house has too much, and has to take something to counteract it — that something being insulin. Insulin burns up the sugar Jacques' metabolism is incapable of consuming. If an unusually large dose of insulin were given to a normal person, obviously the result would be to burn up the essential sugar present, and death would ensue, unless something very speedily supervened. You see how subtly it was thought out. The tampered phial was placed among the others, and it was only a question of time before it was used, it did not matter much when — the murderer would not be there. Even if — and this is the dreadfully cunning part — even if anyone was with her at the time, they would be unable to do anything constructive or preventive unless they knew what had happened — and they couldn't possibly know, of course. They would have to watch her convulsive struggles helplessly until she died; and because she was already ill, the convulsion would most likely merely be taken for another stroke. And so it would have been, but for the unfortunate occurrence of the cat. And the interesting thing is that Jacques' supplies — which must surely be worked out to a dot — began to run short . . . Do you remember telling me that, Miss Brown? That was a bit of a bloomer, wasn't it?'

She wasn't looking at him. Her head

340

was bent over the gibbon she was stroking intently.

'Was it?' she said in a faraway voice. 'I suppose it was.'

'Well, there you are,' said Quentin. 'The whole thing in a tidy nutshell. That was how Julia Jacques was killed. Unrequited love and frustration over a long period combined to determine your intention; you had the chance and you took it; you knew where the insulin was and how to use it; and you believed — quite correctly — that in time Jacques would turn to you for consolation. So far, so good. But I was still not an inch nearer to how or why Raoul was killed. Maybe he suspected the truth and so you had to stop his mouth, to prevent him trying a little gentle blackmail. Yes, it might have been that. But that didn't answer the question — *how?*'

Hattie suddenly raised her head, her pale, slanting eyes staring beyond them all in a kind of frozen ecstasy. Her voice was dry and hoarse.

'I'll tell you. You've guessed so much, I might as well tell you the rest. It was really surprisingly simple and obvious.' She licked her lips. 'Antoine! Will you go to my room? In my desk, you'll find a pigskin wallet with money in it. Bring it to me, will you?'

He looked at her strangely, as though the sight of her made him wince.

'Of course,' he said at last, and turned to go. But someone blocked the doorway, a filthy-looking gnome.

Borodin knocked over his chair in his hurry to get to the door.

'Proo-dance!'

'Hold him, Boris,' said the gnome decisively, and stepped into the room.

'Ah, Miss Whitaker, I didn't recognise you without your glasses. Better late than never. Poor Borodin was getting quite anxious,' said Mr. Seal, not to be outdone in sangfroid.

Borodin stood, obediently clutching Jacques by the arm in the doorway. Hattie stared at them, a dead and hopeless white spreading across her face. The priest and the two Foleys observed all this uncomprehendingly.

Prudence leaned against the table.

'We're sitting on an arsenal,' she remarked. 'The daring of having it right where they lived! It's a wonder it didn't jump to my mind before. These ancient forts nearly always had underground store-rooms, preferably as near ground-level as possible to facilitate replacements. It was probably blocked up and forgotten about until they started building the villa, when they may have accidentally uncovered it. It runs from the rampart steps direct to the creek near the bathing-hut, and inside it's got the sort of lift they have in warehouses, a rough wooden platform on a rope. The store-chambers themselves are chock-full of guns and ammunition: I'll say someone was getting ready for something!'

There was a dazed silence.

'Miss Whitaker has been working on behalf of the British Government for many months now. Quite a dangerous job. They have been aware of the leakage for a long time, and she has been trying to trace its origin all this while. Hence her inexplicable absences and curious secrecy. Now her task is completed, and

343

I'm sure she is very glad,' said Mr. Seal.

'I'll say!' agreed Miss Whitaker, swinging herself on to the table. 'And about time.'

'It's the end of the other crime, too. I was just winding up. Do you mind if I continue?'

'Go ahead,' said Miss Whitaker amiably. 'First come, first served.'

'That was how Raoul was killed,' he announced. 'As Miss Brown said, it was simplicity itself. During those few moments when I was left alone . . . just long enough to dart to the concealed entrance, descend swiftly in the improvised elevator, run out of the creek, stab the boy through the open window, and return the same way. The whole thing wouldn't have taken much more than five minutes.

'It wasn't revenge or jealousy or love that motivated the criminal — it was devastating ambition. Julia was a useless encumbrance. If she were dead, he would be freer and have more money to further his private ends. Like Hattie, he had one end in view for years . . . only his was not

344

the same as hers. Apostle Island was French, ought to belong to the French, and he should be the *Gouverneur*. In a quiet way, he was very popular among the natives, and he was sure that if he brought off a rebellion there were sufficient numbers on his side to make success a certainty. Afterwards, he would indubitably be elected governor.

'I described just now how Julia was killed, while he made a perfect and unbreakable alibi for himself in court. It was a blow that she had willed the money away from him. Such a possibility had never entered his head, so it had not occurred to him to verify it beforehand. A blow, as I said, but it did not radically upset his plans. As the fires of passion died, he had realised that he had chosen the wrong sister to marry; money lasted longer than love. It was a mistake that he intended to rectify as soon as possible. Of course, if he had had the least idea of Hattie's feelings towards him, things might have been very different indeed. As it was, he dared not be too precipitate; a decent amount of time had to elapse after his wife's death before he could hint at his supposed feelings. Meanwhile, a horrid complication arose in the shape of a sudden and wholly unexpected friendship between Hattie and her nephew. He imagined that Hattie had fallen in love with the lad's good looks. To see the two of them together made him sick with rage. He was afraid of saying too much, also. He saw how the boy played up to her, and he knew that Raoul's lust for money was as great, if not greater, than his own. He believed the boy would go to any lengths to obtain the money he wanted. And he hadn't much confidence in Hattie's good sense either. It looked as though all his plans would be ruined.

'According to French law, the law of the Island, an uncle may marry his niece, an aunt her nephew; therefore, *they* could marry, and he was terrified that that was what they intended to do. At all costs that had to be prevented. When he was at the priest's house he abstracted the stiletto. It would do no harm to have it, and if he didn't use it then, it could always find its way back home. If he did use it as a weapon, it was always a help to cast suspicion elsewhere.

'Then, the night I went to dinner with them, he overheard the conversation between his son and his sister-in-law. How much he heard I don't know, but undoubtedly there was something which made him uneasy. He ran his son down as hard as he could over dinner, showing his inconstancy and immorality. Not that he thought it would do much good; he believed it was already too late. At one moment during the meal he went to open the window to the gibbon who was outside. It must have been at that very moment that he saw Raoul, and perhaps Mrs. Foley too, enter the bathing-hut far below. He exclaimed and started back. He was so absorbed by the significance of what he had seen that he hardly opened his mouth during the rest of the meal. Then Hattie left the table, and that was his chance. He made some excuse to me, said he wanted to get some special port, and made his escape. By the secret way, it cannot have taken him more than three minutes to reach his destination, a quick downward thrust in at the window and away again, picking up a bottle of port on his way back and returning to me with scarcely a breath lost. If he was a little paler than usual, it wasn't likely that I would notice it or remember it afterwards. And what an alibi!

'If it had stopped at that, I might have been beaten by it. But the gun-running had to continue. That very night, in fact, a cargo was due, and somehow it had to be prevented. There were too many people and too many inquisitive policemen around just then for it to be safe. Unfortunately for Jacques, Miss Whitaker was on the spot at the very moment when he had to try and warn off the incoming boat. He pretended that he was trying to identify it. But Miss Whitaker, always on the alert for gun-runners — which explains why she was so frequently on the prowl when respectable young ladies are abed — wanted this one to come quietly to shore, her intention being to trap it. Later on, she realised that Jacques was *deliberately* frustrating this and signalling an alarm, and as soon as she knew this, she understood why.

'The cargo was lost that time. Perhaps Borodin wasn't very expert; he may not have had much experience at it. One cargo lost and another picked up by the Patrollers; not a very good record. Jacques *must* have been annoyed. However, he could trust Borodin to hold his tongue, though not indefinitely. Although in the ordinary way such a case would not have come before him, he made it his business to see that this one did. He let him off lightly by ordering him to be deported as soon as possible. That would get him safely out of the way, and there were always plenty of beachcombers ready to take on his job — for a price.'

Suddenly, unexpectedly, Hattie gave a piercing scream, and every head turned for an instant in her direction. Just long enough for Jacques to swing round and drive his fist into the pit of Boris's stomach. Instinctively, Boris let go his arm in order to clutch defensively at his vitals. Jacques was then out of the door and running down the corridor with the clumsy, thunderous tread of a man unused to athletics.

'It's all right,' said Seal, 'Napoleon will get him. He's at the door.'

There was yelling, and somebody calling insistently, and then feet running again on stone. They crowded to the windows to see, by the light of the late afternoon sun, Jacques thudding towards the walls of the ramparts a yard or two ahead of the policeman. He clambered to the top of the wall and stood there panting an instant. He cast a look over his shoulder at his pursuer.

'Antoine!' screeched Hattie. 'No! Don't let him . . . '

One minute he stood there, a thin dark shape against the westering sun. The next, he had thrown up his arms and disappeared . . .

There was a frightening silence . . . Slowly, they moved away from the windows one by one. Hattie, her two attempts at saving him having failed, collapsed in a huddle on the ground, Orlando moaning and plucking at her anxiously.

'It is probably better this way,' said Mr.

Seal at last 'He was a judge. He knew the law. A nasty merciless crime. He knew just what chance he stood if he went to trial, and that was his answer.'

The Foleys, very subdued, went away, both of them rather moved by the secret defence each had made for the other when it became necessary. Miss Whitaker put Miss Brown to bed with a sedative. Father Xavier remained talking to Borodin, trying to find a solution for him — for the deportation papers had been served on him, and the judge's death would not alter the sentence. Brigadier Orage, having collected what remained of the shattered body from the rocks below, was making out his final report with Mr. Seal.

The grimy gnome was back in the room.

'I would have liked to have a bath but there wasn't the time to spare. So much still to be done before the boat sails. Do you mind, Father?'

'Are you leaving, Proo-dance?' said Boris, in his most discouraged voice.

'Certainly. My job here is over, thank

the Lord. We're bound for Nicaragua . . .
Are you ready, Father?'

Father Xavier smiled happily.

'Indeed I am . . . Will these two
gentlemen act as witnesses?' addressing
Seal and the policeman.

The two gentlemen would.

Everyone looked at Boris expectantly,
who returned their gaze blankly.

'Hasn't any one told him?' said Father
Xavier, with a smothered chuckle.

Prudence clapped her dirty paw to her
mouth.

'I declare I clean forgot! Honestly,
there's been such an amount to see to,
what with arranging things with you,
Father, and the F.I. chap in Nicaragua,
and getting temporary papers — not to
mention this jolly little business with its
coincident ramble in the arsenal . . . ' She
turned to Boris nervously. 'I — I've got a
sort of a job for you, Boris, through a
man I know in Nicaragua; it's in the
foreign intelligence. Of course it isn't
anything much to start with, but you've
got the chance of making good. I've got
you a permit to go out there, and once

you're there we can easily get you new papers.'

'We?' said Boris.

'I should have told you before, of course,' she said apologetically. 'Perhaps the idea doesn't appeal to you.' She didn't look at him. 'Of course it means respectability. We'd have to — get married . . . '

'Married!' echoed Boris stupidly. 'Why? You and I?'

Prudence said to the others in a voice that tried to sound amused:

'I suppose the idea of marrying a British agent is too shocking to his ideals.'

'Does she mean it?' growled Boris. And, at their amused assent, suddenly came to life. 'Proo-dance!' he roared ecstatically, like a passionate bear, and seized her in his embrace. 'For you I will even be respectable!'

Demurely, the forlorn maiden turned her grubby face upward until the tattered man's lips pressed on hers . . .